AUGUST, OCTOBER

AUGUST, OCTOBER

ANDRÉS BARBA

*Translated from the Spanish by
Lisa Dillman*

Hispabooks Publishing, S. L.
Madrid, Spain
www.hispabooks.com

Copyright © 2010 by Andrés Barba

Originally published in Spain as *Agosto, Octubre* by Anagrama, 2010
First published in English by Hispabooks, 2015
English translation copyright © by Lisa Dillman
Design © simonpates - www.patesy.com

ISBN 978-84-943658-1-2 (trade paperback)
ISBN 978-84-943658-2-9 (ebook)
Legal Deposit: M-17220-2015

Esta obra ha sido publicada con una subvención
del Ministerio de Educación, Cultura y Deporte de España

The author would like to express his gratitude for the grant received from the HALMA network during the editing phase of this novel, and to thank to the Spanish Ministry of Culture, the Cervantes Institute, the Het Beschrijf literary society in Brussels, and the Translators' House of the Hungarian Ministry of Culture.

For Eduardo Lostao

PART ONE
MEMORY OF AUGUST

It would start on the way from the beach to the house, walking back with his parents and his little sister. Arousal that was more like discomfort than pleasure. He'd take off his bathing suit and masturbate in the bathroom before showering, conjuring up vague images he'd seen on the beach a few minutes earlier or on the walkway that led from the beach to the house his parents had rented for the summer, images that were almost abstract, of girls his age or a little older, sixteen or seventeen. Rather than any one specific body, what he saw when he closed his eyes and began touching himself was an indistinct amalgam of imaginary bodies whose contours were, at the same time, somehow disturbingly concrete. The crease of a girl's hips when she sat, for example, or the slope of breasts in profile, or those strange, circular, dimple-like indentations at the base of a back. He didn't feel attracted to those things, it was more an enthralled sort of revulsion, as if the images somehow merited awe and yet were simultaneously preposterous. Sometimes he actually found it difficult to recall specific bodies he'd just seen, or he could recall them but not tell them apart. He'd have the whitewashed image of a girl in a bikini walking along the water's edge as if her hip hurt with each step, or a girl's back, a skinny back, like that of a sickly old man, or a pair of arms crossed over a chest and an almost amphibian whiteness, full of little, blue veins. He wasn't even thinking about them, exactly, when he masturbated. It felt more like being underwater, like something abating and then welling up, and then receding without having been even remotely resolved. He'd breathe in and out, in and out. Then wipe himself off with toilet paper, wipe the floor, look in the mirror.

"You've changed so much this year," Aunt Eli had said the minute she saw him that summer. "You've become a man all of a sudden."

He'd become a man all of a sudden. In the past six months he'd had such a growth spurt that half his wardrobe no longer fit. His father attributed it to the fact that he'd gotten involved in sports, and he himself was so fascinated by the transformation that ever since his father had made that comment, he'd redoubled his interest in physical activity. His face had grown sharper, his lips had stopped being so fleshy and gotten thinner—like his mother's—his cheekbones protruded, too, as did his chin, which, together with his round, childlike eyes, gave his face a frightened-boy look. He was aware of this effect and so, over the course of that year, had developed the nervous habit of narrowing his eyes when spoken to, as though displeased or mulling something over. His arms had gotten longer, and his legs, but exercise had made them sinewy. He was proud of his arms, but less so his legs, since they were still thin and in all likelihood— at least judging by his father's anatomy—would remain that way for the rest of his life. His chest seemed stuck in an inexplicable, childlike state despite all the exercise, a bit sunken in. Taller than average, he was wiry, though not noticeably so. He knew he wasn't objectively good-looking but also knew that his solemnity and silent demeanor made him seem attractive. Plus, that year he'd become a strong person. Strong in a way that perhaps not even he had imagined he ever would be. He'd borne his scrawny childhood and adolescence like some sort of Biblical plague. In the same way an ugly girl looks in the mirror and thinks crossly *this is not me*, he had looked in the mirror for years and felt a sort of furious discord between what he was and what he saw. A month after turning fourteen, he realized, astonished, how much he'd changed, and he felt as if a dull fury were subsiding, as if some nebulous clot had dissolved, and he clenched his jaw.

"And that's not all," his mother said. "If you could see how organized he's become . . ."

Aunt Eli had given him a babyish cuddle and a noisy smack, provoking his instant displeasure. Order and cleanliness were actually like overspill from his physical change. He'd become methodical and meticulous, as if he felt the need to follow a step-by-step plan to the letter.

"I don't know what happened to him. You know how messy he used to be, and then from one day to the next . . ."

He hated that about his mother, the relentless habit she had of talking about him to other people as if he weren't there, and the fact that she was doing it with Aunt Eli irked him especially. Maybe it was his mother's uncanny ability to make him revert into a five-year-old with a single look, or maybe it was the objective shame of someone feeling constantly on the verge of being exposed that drove him crazy. Aunt Eli sat down beside him and scooted in close. He felt her enormous breasts spilling over his shoulder, and this time he couldn't help but be disgusted. He pulled away, grimacing involuntarily. Not even in illness had she been able to lose weight, but she had become very pale, and the result was that rather than a real person, she now resembled an enormous wax figure, white and doughy.

"So, you're a young man now, huh? Don't even want to cuddle. Or you do, but not with your Aunt Eli . . ."

"I'm going to my room," he said, bouncing up like a spring, and before he'd even managed to leave the room, he heard his mother offering feeble excuses and Aunt Eli empathizing.

"Oh, it's normal, dear . . ."

Each summer they rented a different house, and that summer's was the nicest one they'd had in a long time, an old, two-story bungalow very close to the beach. It had four bedrooms upstairs—which meant that for the first time he didn't have to share a room with his sister for the summer—and a huge, wrap-around balcony with bamboo blinds that could be rolled up with little cords and then tied to the balcony's supporting columns. When they walked in the first day, it was all he could do to keep from shouting in glee. It looked like an African house, an explorer's refuge. The first floor was open-plan, designed the way houses on the estuary often are, on stilts to avoid flooding. They were old fishermen's quarters that had been renovated into luxury vacation homes for city folks—carefully restored inside, though the decorators had cleverly preserved some of the "original charming inconveniences" (Mamá). They spent the first few days enjoying the house with almost angst-ridden delight. Deep down they were a childish family. Just as some families were melancholy, or happy, or destructive, theirs was a childish family. They got overexcited at the drop of a hat, then grew sad for no reason. They needed swift kicks for motivation, especially in the summer, and then felt their joy simply wither and rushed on, with bold and terrifying logic, to another form of entertainment, as if the whole point of summer were to flee the tedium of their previous hobbies. They were as disorderly in the summertime as they were orderly in the winter. The rest of the year, his father ran a banking firm, his mother, a pharmacy in the

city center, and he and his sister went to school;
they were reasonable and hardworking, not
overly emotional, and a bit reclusive, but there
was a healthy air of calm at home. Summer,
though, was the time for anarchy. They all got
a little impatient, a little selfish, were lively and
happy most of the time, but also more prone
to disappointment and tantrums. They fought
more, but also confided in each other more and
enjoyed spending time together. Summer was
also the season of every moment of genuinely
transfixed joy he could recall, of dinners when
all four of them would suddenly fall silent as
if something were bubbling up inside them,
or propelling them forward in life, their voices
growing deep and calm. He'd always yearned
for summer with real excitement, and it seemed
strange to him that it had been different that
year. The month before their trip, for the first
time in years, his father brought up the
possibility of going someplace new for their
summer vacation. The issue was discussed at
dinner over the course of a couple of weeks, but
then Aunt Eli got sick and that was the end of
that—they'd go the same place as always. He
felt affronted more than anything by the fact
that no one had asked his opinion, but the
affront quickly morphed into a strange and

still-new feeling, a sort of disillusionment with his parents, a resentful disappointment; they struck him as simpletons, as doormats. Then came a very bitter dinner, two weeks before they were to leave, during which they fought intensely. Their argument lasted several minutes, growing progressively louder, and culminating in his calling Aunt Eli "a sick cow." He knew that what had provoked his insult wasn't animosity toward his aunt—whom he really did love sincerely—but a sort of impetuous urge; the desire to call Aunt Eli *a sick cow* right in the middle of a family dispute was too new and compelling to go unheeded. In a fraction of a second, fleeting and almost irresistible thoughts darted through his mind, and in the end he was unable to resist the impulse to see what result a comment like that would have. More than insulting Aunt Eli, he wanted to incite the aftermath of the insult. He half-stood, hands on the table, and said, "I'm not spending my summer taking care of some sick cow."

He remembered the words flowing from his mouth like liquid, something thick yet fluid. He might have been shocked at how easy it was. He wanted to be risky, to jeopardize everything. His father banged a sonorous fist down on the table, and he himself marched out of the dining room. The conclusion was even sorrier. His mother came into his room, acting as a mediator, and asked with concern why he'd said that, begged him to apologize to his father. He remembered that he'd been sitting on his bed and his mother had sat down beside him and stroked his neck, and that without wanting to, he'd blushed. He got up and returned to the dining room, apologized without looking his father in the eyes and without knowing whether he felt humiliated or just tense, and when he looked up he saw them both— his father still glowering at him, his mother standing beside him, looking startled. He wasn't sure why, but he stopped seeing them, then, as he'd seen them his whole life, they were no longer symbols of authority, were no longer bathed in the benevolent glow of childhood, no longer superior beings; they, too, had been strangely degraded somehow. It was as though he'd discovered in them phony, unsophisticated attributes. They looked, there in the harsh light of normality, like a couple of milksops, full of fear or repressed passions.

The fight was soon forgotten, and that also disappointed him a bit; he'd become stubborn that year. They were in good moods on the train ride down, and when they arrived at the house they'd rented, their happiness made them relaxed and chatty for a few days, and then the troubling phase set in. They'd go to the beach in the morning, and on their way back to the house for lunch, he'd scan the pine trees lining the walkway, the dunes, the bodies of girls his age and of older women.

He went for a run on the beach almost every day. He loved running by the sea. At times he felt his body was a machine over which he had some sort of total control; it was a way to release the shame he was overcome by again and again and for no reason. When he got back to his parents' beach umbrella, he'd toss his T-shirt down and go in the water, by the rocks where his mother and sister hunted for crabs. On their fifth day of vacation, when he came back from his run, he dove into the water as he did every day and felt a strange temptation—he'd plunged in without taking a big breath first, but once underwater he decided to swim to a rock about ten feet below the surface, where he saw something that looked like coral. He took two or three erratic strokes, but then halfway down he reached out for the side of the rock and grabbed hold of it. And once there, he decided to hold his breath for as long as he could. The rock was rough and black, and when he lodged his shoulder beneath its ledge to keep himself from floating back to the surface, he found he had almost no air left and knew he couldn't last more than three or four seconds. And then he felt as if something were breaking—some resistance maybe, or fear—and it occurred to him that he could die there, and the idea didn't frighten him in the slightest. He recalled the muffled, silent sound of the water during those seconds, and that he'd kept his eyes open. The seafloor, which must have been about thirty feet down and had first looked clear, turned a bit blurry. Looking up he saw the water's luminous surface. He had almost no air left, and it looked staggeringly beautiful, as if it had turned into impenetrable glass. Then he felt like the water was getting thicker, thick as oil, and darker, too. Having surpassed what he thought was the limit of his resistance, he was flooded with a strange, mysterious sense of relief, as though his blood had reoxygenated. How much time had elapsed? He had no way of knowing, but that brief euphoria was followed by an immediate weakness and the feeling that everything was about to turn white, that the darkness of the seafloor would light up with a sinister glow. He wrenched his shoulder from beneath the rock ledge and with the last of his strength took a single stroke toward the surface. When he burst through the water, he gulped the air furiously, not knowing whether what filled his chest was pleasure or pain, and realized he was going to lose consciousness. He didn't know how he managed to get back to the top of the rock. He fainted there. The next thing he remembered was being at the Red Cross clinic, and when he opened his eyes, he saw his father standing beside him.

"You gave us a real scare," he said.

His father's face was contorted, as though he'd had an unthinkable fright. He was very pale, and when he stroked his face—an act he began with confidence and then became embarrassed by for some reason—he could feel his hand trembling.

"Your mother and sister are outside. Everything's OK. It's a good thing this fellow here saw you."

"Manuel," said an impressively athletic young man who looked about thirty, standing beside his father with a satisfied expression.

"Manuel, yes, I'm sorry."

Manuel seemed to feel the need to make some sort of statement, and since no one thanked him, he did it himself, mentally, and then answered aloud.

"It was nothing. What matters is that you're OK."

That episode was followed by a melancholy afternoon. What had happened? A thing with no name. His breathing was a bit labored, and he felt weak. Anita was solicitous, as if she were the older sibling for a day and he the younger one. He lay in the hammock on the balcony and watched her come and go, asking every fifteen minutes if he wanted a glass of water or anything. She was wearing a red summer dress from which her pudgy little legs stuck out like two reeds. It was almost heartbreaking. For several hours he seemed to have lost the ability to have normal emotions proceed one after the other. He felt drowsy but had sudden fits of unease, or anguish, he couldn't pay attention to anything and yet there was a sort of constant thought or sound or music there, something almost intangible, a sort of fear assaulting him from outside, fear of the thing he'd almost done and that he still didn't fully understand.

His parents spent all evening encouraging him to go to the beach club the next day to see if any of his friends from previous summers had arrived yet. They seemed unconvinced that what had happened on the beach had simply been an accident, especially his father, and it was as though they'd conspired to ensure he wouldn't be on his own for even a minute.

"We can both go tomorrow, together, if you want," he said.

And then his mother, "But what happened, exactly? You suddenly got dizzy, that's it? Maybe we should take you to the doctor, you've never had dizzy spells in your life!"

And Anita's eyes suddenly brimmed with tears; she'd been holding them in all through lunch, staring at him with strange, dreamlike intensity, and when his mother brought up the doctor, her eyes filled with tears and she began to cry convulsively, as if someone were shaking her body, making it jerk. She took a tiny step toward him, longing to be touched, but it was her mother who hugged her.

"It's all over now, silly. Why would you cry now? Can't you see your brother's fine?"

But he was the only one who seemed to realize how much it bothered Anita to be called silly, how her forehead scrunched up in something that wasn't pain, or a release of tension, but wounded pride, pure and simple—diminutive pride, wounded, in that diminutive body.

"I'm not silly," she said.

Anita.

Their summers had a strangeness to them, a tendency to be compartmentalized, filled with identical activities, there was a sort of routine to their relaxation into which new and extravagant plans were sometimes introduced ("How would you like to try water skiing?"—Papá), white noise, bedrooms they'd never again inhabit but which for that one month took on all the easy-going languor of intimacy, almost like a whisper, so it was as though they'd already been in those exact same circumstances countless times, and yet they were entirely new, the pine trees looking different depending on the view from the house, and also the dunes that hid their view of the shore from the balcony; only occasionally did their wintertime lives occur to them at all, and even then it was a struggle to recall them. Sometimes the sensation of summertime was purely auditory—an inflection in the air that made them breathe a certain way, slower—or it was the easy lethargy of their movements at mealtimes, as though they couldn't be bothered to complete any of their gestures. If he stopped to consider all the summers of his life and compared them to that one, he could immediately see that there was a before and after with regard to the episode at the beach. Up until that day, that particular summer hadn't seemed much different from the others; afterward, it had taken on unprecedented velocity.

He'd wake up early. The same morning his father made him go to the beach club to meet up with his supposed friends from previous summers, for instance, he'd gotten up at seven, had breakfast alone in the kitchen, and then puttered around the house. He stole one of his father's cigarettes and went out to the balcony to smoke it. He didn't smoke often, but it was a custom he enjoyed, and he always did it alone, for fear of looking stupid. His parents' room opened onto the balcony, and they'd slept with the window open. He peeked in and saw them lying in bed, not touching, his father on his back, in his underwear, his mother curled in a ball, her nightgown bunched between her legs. He'd seen them asleep many times, and they hardly looked any different that morning from the way he remembered, but on other occasions he'd felt almost embarrassed and left right away, and that morning he stood gazing at them for some time. He confirmed what he'd often suspected—that their faces got puffy while they slept, that their bodies were appreciably fuller and heavier than during the day, and drier, too, as though something dehydrated them in the night. He actually had to force himself to hold his gaze on them for so long. At first he felt an ordinary embarrassment and the urge to turn away, but soon he got the strange impression that he was appropriating something private, something that was somehow wrong of him to see despite the fact that it happened every day. It was as if they were almost chalky, almost obese, like a couple of puppets worse for wear—they looked like they'd been stuffed with cotton, bounced off the walls and ceiling a thousand times, and had then collapsed atop the bed like that, the backs of his mother's knees full of tiny, blue and deep-red veins, the skin on his father's belly thin and delicate, like an old man or a very old dog—their breathing was deep, something had been lapping at them in the night, or maybe their whole lives.

Later, when they'd finished breakfast and his father suggested they go to the beach club, he eyed him watchfully. From below, his profile was still majestic; he walked amiably and was less puffy than when he was asleep, but he also looked more agile, more virile. All his life, he'd admired his father's grace, and now he was discovering—as though the discovery had occurred while watching him sleep but taken until that moment to be confirmed—that he was also a troubled man, biased, impatient, perhaps sensual; he was discovering that his grace was the result of pretense, a pretense as ingrained as a habit or an incurable defect.

"Did you have any girlfriends before Mamá?"

"Where did that come from?" his father asked, turning to him, bemused.

"Just curious, I guess." He kicked a stick to divert attention, and because he regretted having brought it up. They'd never confided in one another and were bad at it, both of them immediately self-conscious.

"Sure. Lots. One for quite a long time. A friend of your Aunt Eli's."

"So why'd you break up?"

"Because I met your mother. And because you and your sister were destined to be born, I guess."

He smiled when he finished speaking, as though feeling the need to apologize for that nod to sentimentality. His father's genuine amiability did not in fact extend to the realm of intimacies. He was an affable man, an extrovert in the superficial sense of the word, but as quiet as dark waters. Only occasionally did his emotions erupt, like a sudden flowering of some sort, so this expression of optimistic fatalism seemed surprising; he was like the "ideal father" but with a key attribute missing. Floating within him was something akin to a lack.

"I'll come get you around lunchtime, if you want—that way you'll have time to catch up with everyone."

"OK."

But he didn't even go in. He stood for a second and watched his father walk toward the beach, then headed for the estuary. What lingered in his mind when he thought about the kids he'd hung out with other summers was something between never-ending humiliation and a blanket tedium that was exhausting. They were boys and girls from good families—almost all from the city—and they behaved like mini-emperors, a plague of fourteen-year-old serpents, green and shiny, taking over that small beach town every summer. Over the course of the previous summer, he'd begun to experience a strange feeling of contempt for them, embarrassed on their behalf but also overcome by a vague sense of inadequacy. They were almost all good looking, almost all blond or nearly blond, and they made him aware of their beauty and affluence in a relentless and particularly unpleasant way, as if he and all those whose presence was not smarmily justified should revolve around them like satellites in the hopes of falling into their good graces at some point. Their actual behavior was fairly passive, but they took for granted that the world existed to serve them, and when they wanted something, they simply took it. Perhaps what humiliated him the most about the whole situation was that he'd once been spellbound by them, that he'd tried to belong, to join their group. He was like a spiteful girlfriend, and his animus—an animus he felt in his stomach, bitter, pulsating, unresolved, like that of a person ashamed at having loved another—was perhaps fierier than strictly reasonable.

He headed for the estuary, because the estuary was where you weren't supposed to go. The area beyond the houses and the three apartment blocks was forbidden territory. When coming in from the highway, you went through that part of town. The houses were flat and square, like cardboard boxes stacked up by a dumpster ("They should just get rid of all those people."—Mamá); he had a few memories, some fixed, others fluid, as though something in them had turned liquid as they passed by— three men standing by a door talking, a bunch of kids, beat-up old pick-up trucks—there was something sad and violent about it, albeit without any visible signs of violence ("And where would you suggest putting them? It's not like they're hurting anyone."—Papá), and people said that was where all the drug trafficking went on, but drugs, too, were a far-off place, an event difficult to imagine, something vertical atop the squashed-down horizontality of those houses, as if drugs rained down from the sky like brimstone.

The morning heat became palpable as he continued walking in that direction, and when he crossed the vacant lot separating the last few buildings from those houses, he recalled that the previous summer, Aunt Eli mentioned that a man had turned up dead there. By the lot was a pine grove not very different from the one separating their house from the beach; there, however, the stumpy pines on the marshland looked more gnarled, squatter, as though stunted by some nefarious earth-force. He didn't know what he was hoping to find; he was trying to translate it into words, but he'd always been better at feeling than thinking. He even said it aloud—"A dead man." But nothing happened.

When he was just two hundred yards or so from the houses, he saw them in the distance, heading toward town, toward him. It had occurred to him that he'd end up bumping into them at some point. From the distance they looked older than they in fact turned out to be. There were four of them, two were shirtless and all four wore long swim trunks. The last rational thought he had was that if he turned around right then and started running for the buildings, they wouldn't be able to catch him, but rather than do that, he bent and picked up a rock the size of his hand and kept going. When he was twenty or so yards away, he saw them talking amongst themselves, and when he was just five yards away, they stood blocking his path. He didn't examine their faces closely, and in fact they all looked to him like a single, dark, almost black mass; individually, none of them was stronger than he was, and although they were his age, they seemed slightly older because they were tough.

"Where you off to, princess?"

"Just taking a walk."

"All by your lonesome?"

He didn't know how it seemed to other people, but to him violence was something akin to a weather condition inside your skull, a certain quality to the air, something dry and crackly and electric. Sometimes he seemed to go looking for it without meaning to, other times it seemed to hound him, closing in and wreaking havoc on his senses, the single most unfailing instinct, the most instinctual of all instincts. In a flash, muscles tensed, a decision was made, and it was too late to stop anything. There was something almost sensual about it, not so much the actual event (he'd only been in three fights in his life, and all three had been over in a flash) but the build-up; violence, really, was a drawn-out endeavor, fights were won or lost long before they took place, in the dance of glances, tension, hesitation. When he looked again at their faces, they seemed more aggressive than before. He felt unsure of his chances, but also excited by the fact that they hadn't already pummeled him.

"I've got a rock here. The first one to come at me gets his nose broken. You'll probably kill me after that, but over my dead body, one of you is going home with a broken nose."

"Break *his*—wouldn't be the first time."

"Why don't you let him break yours, you fucking asshole?" the other kid replied.

They were silent for an instant. If the situation wasn't resolved immediately, he thought, he didn't stand a chance. They were still unruffled, but he was increasingly nervous. Then suddenly he became afraid. He felt like one of his legs was trembling and pressed it harder into the ground so they wouldn't be able to tell. It was true, one of them did have a smashed-looking nose. The stockiest one crouched down and picked up a rock, too, almost as big as his.

"Look, princess—now I got a rock, too. What if I break yours instead?"

"Hey," another kid said, "I like your T-shirt. Can I have it?"

"No."

"Selfish," he retorted, mockingly. "No need to be so selfish . . ."

He felt them edge closer. His mind was nearly blank. His hands were shaking, and he felt his face turn pale, and then red, and then even redder. In a way he was proud of himself, but he was also so scared that he worried he'd be unable to control his own reactions from one second to the next. He knew he had to strike first; it didn't matter what happened after that, he had to strike first. He took a step forward, but then suddenly hesitated and the biggest kid shoved him hard, causing him to fall onto his back. He leapt up and grabbed the legs of the first boy he could, pulling him to the ground. He heard one of them speak.

"Wait, let's see what he does."

And in a flash he grabbed the neck of the kid he'd pulled down. He immediately realized he was the stronger of the two but was afraid they'd all dive in. Grabbing him in a chokehold, he saw his face, which looked haloed in white; he was panting. The kid was weirdly ugly, with a strange upper lip, like a harelip. Little by little, vacillating, he loosened his grip and then stood. He was sweating profusely. He stood there as if to say *who's next?* It was clear he didn't have a chance against the stocky one.

"Not bad," said the kid who looked the oldest, smiling sort of scornfully. And then, after a brief silence, "Hey."

"What?"

"Come with us."

"Where to?"

"The dock, to go swimming."

There came another moment of indecision, of incredulity, and then he rattle-laughed, as though hit by machine-gun fire. He saw them smile—all but the kid he'd knocked down, who was still massaging his neck and pissed off. Violence was a psychological game, too, a motor. The piston generated a spark and after the explosion, it released hot, heavy air.

"OK, I don't have anything else to do," he replied.

So, those were the kids from the dock. He'd already seen them several times over the course of that first week and longed to join them but at the last minute had always been overcome by shyness. Sometimes he lacked the final push it took to make up his mind to actually do things, as though his brain worked faster than his desires and handed him everything already carefully and thoroughly digested; he could live with tension and fervor, and handle situations that demanded speed and skill, but not those that required strategy—that was when he became nervous and impatient.

"What are your names?"

"Pablo."

"Tejas."

"Rivero."

And when the fourth boy did not answer, the last to speak added, "That's Marcos."

Their voices had a different tenor somehow—intimate, like wood grain. Seen from up close, they now took on their own individual characteristics, but they all still had something in common, too, as though their beauty emanated from their discontent, from their anger. Marcos was blond, skin and bones, and his lip gave him the surly air of an ex-convict; he had a jerky, flailing bounce to

his step, as though through sheer agitation
something inside him had gotten tangled
up. Pablo and Tejas, sinewy as two nerves,
looked so much alike that he thought they
were brothers that first day. They were the
happiest and most sarcastic of the group, and
also the calmest. Rivero was the brawniest
and the only objectively attractive one of the
four—like a new and improved model. They
couldn't have been more than fourteen, and yet
they were older than him, as old as fossil fish,
as survival, as torture or neglect. They'd become
realists. Their sexuality was clearly developed,
and that seemed to have created mysterious
bonds among them, a closeness and empathy,
like wolves that went hunting in a pack.

"What about you, princess, what's your
name?"

"Tomás."

"Tomás," Rivero repeated.

"Yeah. Tomás."

"Ever had your dick sucked, Tomás?"

He looked down, clenched his jaw, and when
he turned back to Rivero, he squinted his eyes
as hard as he could. They were almost to the
dock.

"Once."

"Once?"

"Yeah."

Suddenly he felt a huge hand clamp down on his neck from behind. It was Rivero, and his hand was a show of force. He wrenched away in pain.

"Don't lie to me, faggot. I know perfectly well when I'm being lied to."

Then he smiled.

Two full weeks of vacation remained. He felt that calm euphoria of having won something. At home he became sullen, presumptuous, independent. He'd see his parents and Anita, and they were sort of distant, irritating figures. He no longer bothered to smile. When he was with them, he was a little absent ("Son, you're unbearable this summer."—Mamá), but he let them be, spent time with them when required and then took off as soon as he could, giving no other explanation than that he was going to the club. But he didn't go to the club. He had the vague feeling—he could have called it happiness, but it was constantly contorting, changing shape and appearance—that a magnetic field had been erected around him. Six days had passed since he met the boys, and he'd gone to see them every single afternoon. He'd gotten to know them a little better and sensed between them an almost physical connection, as though they were all keeping a secret, or maybe more than one. Theirs was a solemn world, an adult world, but in certain things they were unable to avoid a few traits that had spilled over from childhood, as though they could only be adult at certain times or when doing certain things. He realized almost immediately, for instance, that they were nearly entirely oblivious of the future, and that in that regard he was far superior. They lived in a kind of exhausting, ever-repeated present. They usually went first to the dock and then into town. Their presence made the only commercial street in town even louder and more colorful. They lived there all year long and assured him that in the winter there wasn't a soul around, which was almost hard to believe now, in summertime. They stole cheap jewelry and T-shirts and paper cones full of shrimp in an astonishingly natural way, and then left them half-eaten, or contemptuously tossed down whatever they'd taken. It wasn't hard to steal, and in fact they seemed almost bored by it, which made it a fascinating spectacle. He himself had stolen on occasion—in the city, in small shops—and had always gotten wildly panicked about it. He had such an ingrained sense of possession that he was incapable of taking anything he didn't really and truly covet. But these kids stole indiscriminately, in a confident and irrational manner, and they took the most absurd, useless objects. What's more, they did it with extraordinary languor. They didn't even pretend to be debating whether or not to buy something, and at times didn't even bother to hide it before walking out of the store. Their movements were so forthright and unequivocal that the first time Pablo stole a pair of earrings in front of him, he was so casual that if anyone had asked about his friend on the way out, he couldn't have said for sure whether or not he'd paid. He didn't even revel in his success afterward. Instead he simply announced, "For Moni."

"Whatever, man, you're still not going to fuck her, even in your dreams."

"We'll see."

And the way they talked about sex was the same as the way they stole. There was something novel about it, about their way of talking about sex, and not just because they were more precocious than he was. He had city friends who were more precocious than him, too, but their attitude was very different. Besides, he himself had had the chance to lose his virginity a few months earlier and had passed it up for lack of interest and because he just wasn't that into the girl. Marcos, Pablo, Tejas, and Rivero talked about sex in a clinical, neutral way. Despite the fact that it was a constant and explicit topic of conversation, there was something underneath it that they were somehow avoiding. The girls they slept with lived in the same boxy houses as they did, and they'd slept with many of the same ones. They didn't brag, but nor did they skip over embarrassing, even sordid, details. It was as though the act of fucking or being fucked were just that, as though it were simply a basic, vital thing, ever-present in the world of possibilities—a perpetual fervor, but one that had no object, or whose object was met by virtue of the act itself, only to then start up once again, unrelenting. Sex wasn't sentimental— they didn't talk about falling in love or about thinking about any one girl in particular, they talked about fucking, how bad they wanted to fuck, how long it had been since they'd fucked, Moni giving good head, Duli taking it up the ass, they remarked casually that they'd fucked Frani in her father's pick-up truck (and once— Tejas—even Frani's mother). All the girls had nicknames ending in *i*, and that seemed their only nod to sentimentality; everything else was relentless tension, risk. Fucking, getting fucked, there was no drama, no disobedience, no lying, they were not caught—as he and his city friends were—in a web of phony soulfulness, weren't obliged to pretend; their tension came of something more painful, but also nobler, or at least that's the way it seemed to him.

He started to feel he'd been lied to all his life. It wasn't so much a concrete thought, more a strange sort of clairvoyance. He knew, too, that he'd never be like them, like Pablo, Marcos, Tejas, and Rivero, but he was happy enough to be liked by them and sensed they were proud to have him around, to tease him a little, but not cruelly. He felt like a bridge between two worlds; they felt like the pauper who somehow manages, one wondrous night, to sleep with a model.

"It's one of the wonders of the world," Aunt Eli said.

"What is?"

"The Eiffel Tower. I don't want to die without seeing the Eiffel Tower."

"Oh, please, Eli, it's not like you're going to die tomorrow."

"You don't know that, maybe I *will* die tomorrow. I'd like to see it, I've never traveled anywhere in my whole life."

Aunt Eli made the first pronouncement with an alarming degree of authority and the second as though attempting to quell the tremors produced by the first. And then, ten minutes later, during the same dinner, "I'd have been happier married to a Turk."

And then later still, while discussing how the ocean was warmer that summer than it had been other summers, "No one has ever loved me, my whole life." (There ensued a deadly silence, followed by a pained *come on, what are you talking about, Eli?* from his father.) Something about Aunt Eli had changed that summer, and that was the precise dinner that he noticed it—a sort of verbal toughness (she, who had never been tough about anything her whole life), as though she were trying to wrench things from her mouth, incomplete things, unfulfilled things, things that served no purpose but had been shut away in a sort of internal locker, a locker as large as her body.

"You have your family, your job in the city, you don't know what it's like, living in a small town, you don't know a thing. This town is a graveyard."

Then she turned to his father and to them, her expression calm, almost as though she were surprised or thinking *why don't any of you understand me?* and announced, "I used to be very pretty, do you remember?"

"Of course I remember."

"I was very pretty, for how long? Ten years? I should have taken advantage of it at the time. Sometimes I think you get to a crossroads in life—one way," she pointed with a pudgy hand, "and another way," and with the opposite hand she gestured in the other direction. "But you need a third option, the real one, the one that's not offered; you do what you think you want, and it's never really what you wanted, and in the end you lose your talent."

Later, in the kitchen, while his parents were clearing the dishes, he overheard his mother speaking to his father.

"Your sister is stark raving mad, what's gotten into her?"

"I don't know, I told you yesterday. She's been like this since we got here," his father responded, concerned.

He himself had been so absent the past few evenings that he hadn't realized they'd been discussing it for days. It was obvious, though—something in Aunt Eli had been thrown out of whack. She'd behaved like that throughout dinner, and when they said goodnight and his parents told him to walk her home, she stood for a second at the door, kissed his father, and said simply, "I'm no good at being sick."

And then, to Anita, "Aunt Eli didn't frighten you, did she, Anita?"

Anita fired back with a booming *no!* her eyes screwed tight as pins. It was impossible to know what was going on inside her when she was like that.

Aunt Eli lived almost all the way on the other side of town, in one of the last few houses before those fronting the estuary. It was a Sunday night, and there were very few people on the promenade, plus it was late, because dinner had gone on and on. All of a sudden her body smelled sweet, like cinnamon. He remembered, too, the faint scent of cheap food and talcum powder at her house. It was a small house where she'd lived with her husband for fifteen years until he died. They'd had a prosperous shrimping business for many years and actually owned a small fleet of four boats but lost two of them one day in rough waters, and when it came out that the boats didn't meet all of the safety standards, the families of the fishermen killed in the incident sued. They lost everything they'd saved up over the course of ten years. One of the two remaining boats burned down at the shipbuilder's, while it was being repaired. That left just one, and they never managed to rebuild their business, it just slowly languished. When her husband died, Aunt Eli sold the last boat, the *Lady Pepa II*. He remembered a photo of himself, with Anita when she was a baby, sitting on the *Lady Pepa II*'s nets. As for his uncle, he had only one distinct memory of him, of a day when they spent all afternoon together and he'd crouched down and said, "Now, take a look at this—I bet you've never seen anything like it in your life."

He'd pulled a huge wad of bills out of his pocket and deposited it in his hands.

"Come on, kid, take hold of it, it's not going to bite."

He recalled feeling the unusual weight of that wad of cash in his hands, a weight both inconsequential and unsettling, like that of a sick bird.

"I don't want to keep going to the doctor," Aunt Eli said on their way back to her house, walking along the esplanade. "What can he do for me?"

"I don't know, Aunt Eli."

"Take a good look at me," she said, stopping. "I'm ordinary. I've turned into an ordinary woman. That's the one thing I'll never forgive myself for—having become an ordinary woman. Never turn into an ordinary man."

"I won't."

It was dark out, and hot and muggy. A light breeze jangled the pulleys on the boats moored at the estuary, and the current made them all bob softly, unevenly. Suddenly he was certain he'd think back on that scene in the future, that precise moment—Aunt Eli calling herself an ordinary woman, how pale she was, her illness practically glowing in the night, her head listing forward and rocking back, as though she, too, were affected by the tides. It was weird—in addition to being obese, she also now seemed diminutive. Diminutive and fragile, as though her life were trembling inside her. They walked slowly and didn't speak again until they'd almost reached her house.

"You're up to something; there's a glint in your eye," she said.

"I'm not up to anything."

"You've changed. You've done something, I can see it in your eyes."

He made no reply. He'd never seen Aunt Eli act so bizarrely somber. She, in fact, was the one with a glint in her eyes, the one who seemed to have done something, the one who'd thrown all pleasantries to the wind.

"You're just like your father when he was your age."

"I know," he said. He'd seen pictures of his father when he was young and always felt the same self-conscious shame, as though he were walking a straight line originally laid down by his father's body, in black-and-white, so like his own. He didn't like to be reminded of it. He waggled his head and squinted his eyes to shake off the likeness.

"First you'll be restless, then you'll calm down, and in the end you'll become a kind and respectable gentleman. Do you know what you want to study?"

"Architecture."

He'd been saying "architecture" for two years, an automatic response even though he'd actually stopped wanting it some time ago. It was a quick reply, one that put an immediate end to the conversation, bestowing a halo of awe on him for such precocity. He liked coming off as precocious and interesting, and architecture was the most exotic subject he'd been able to think of.

"You don't look like an architect," Aunt Eli declared.

"No?"

"No, you've got too much spirit."

When he kissed her goodbye, he was surprised at how cold her skin felt, but his shock lasted only an instant, and as he walked back home, he strolled slowly, flattered by what Aunt Eli had said. So it was visible, he thought, the fact that he had too much spirit was visible. He felt jittery, full of life, though perhaps only due to the contrast—contemplating his own body and spirit and then comparing them to Aunt Eli's. He saw a few girls he thought might be looking at him. He smiled. He almost wanted to turn to them and ask, *Do you like me? Huh? You sort of like me, right?*

There were girls in their crowd, too. Girls who were like the inverse of Pablo, Marcos, Tejas, and Rivero. The first time he saw them by the estuary, their faces, too, had all seemed like one; he'd been with the boys, and they all said hi, walked over, and sat on their towels. How many were there? Seven? Eight? The first day, their faces all blurred together, swimming around him. They must have been thirteen or fourteen years old. As he turned around, he heard one of them ask, "Where'd you get *him*? I'd like to get a taste of *that* . . ."

And Rivero, "He's all yours."

But when he turned to look, there was no one specific face. They looked like a garden, laid out in rows, with an untamed sweetness about them; their bodies weren't exactly slim, weren't like the girls from the club, weren't like those he knew in the city, they had an unfamiliar plumpness, an unfamiliar scent, an unfamiliar texture. Their faces were daring and naïve and silly, their chins round, their arms healthy and firm, their thighs strong, their chests well developed, they produced in him a strange, carnal chafing, they were sweet, clumsy, guileless, giddy, selfish, shrieking. He had the vague, vain impression that any one of them would have taken him, that he could have approached any one of them on one of the few nights left of vacation and said *will you suck my dick?* and that they—their unremarkable features worn as seashells on the shore—would do it, with a bored air, maybe. He didn't especially like any one of them in particular, and yet all together they transported him into an uncharted physical territory. They talked—what did they talk about? It didn't matter.

It was early in the evening, and he realized he had ten days of summer vacation left. The sun was starting to set behind the estuary. Time always seemed frozen at that hour, and it transformed the entire town, making it appear submerged in an orange and pink liquid, and then a bluish, vacation-like one. No one had anywhere to be. The day's heat was dying down, and a comfortable breeze cleansed the air; everything was light. The girls started putting beach wraps and skirts on over their worn-out bikinis.

"You should come to the fair tonight. It just started."

"We might." (Tejas)

"Like you have anything better to do," one of them joked (he'd already forgotten all of their names).

"What do you know?"

"And bring *him*, OK?"

That time, when he turned, he was being devoured by a pair of brown eyes as hard as marbles.

"If he wants to come, you mean."

"Right, if he wants to come," the same voice replied suggestively, but he'd already stopped looking at her. Later, getting ready to go to the fair, before he left the house, he couldn't even remember her face, no matter how titillating the impression she'd made was. He felt he'd behaved timidly, like he hadn't even responded, and he hated himself for it, but her voice was like an image, rippling through him.

"Where are you off to?" (Mamá)

"The fair."

"With the kids from the club?"

"Yeah."

Later at the fair he'd end up unintentionally bumping into them—the kids from the club—but first it was all bright lights. The world at the fair always seemed cagey. Or sad, maybe. All his life, every year, he'd looked forward to the fair as if it were one of the summer's great events, but now, for the first time, it struck him as exceptionally disappointing, melancholy almost. When he walked in, there weren't many people yet; it was early still—the time for families, fussy children, carnival giants with oversized heads, for the raffling off of dried-out hams. Preposterous-sized dolls gazed down from above, noosed and strangled, their eyes gleefully neurotic. As a kid, he'd come many times with his father to the parking lot where the fair was held every year, and every year he'd been proud to walk in with him, jittery with excitement, as though traveling a luminous highway that bisected the middle of a small, dusty town. His father would talk about how it had been when he was young, or he'd bump into a childhood friend who'd comment on how much the two of them resembled one another, and he'd feel honored and enigmatic. His father would tell whoever it was that he was a good kid. That first fair, though, the one from the early days, seemed to have been switched off, and it was no longer a luminous highway but a thinly lit stream, slightly asphyxiating— the charcoal-grilled seafood had a burned smell, and its thick smoke was off-putting; the music was way too loud and awful; from time to time, in little rainbows of light, there appeared the faces of overexcited children having tantrums as they got off rides. Pablo, Marcos, Tejas, and Rivero were already there with the girls. He'd never seen them dressed up for a night out before. The girls were wearing miniskirts or gaudily bright, tight pants; the boys wore black, as though they'd purposely coordinated, and they were in high spirits. He approached them with a condescending air, as though just playing along with some kid's joke; it was as if on that of all nights he wanted to be different from them, and he didn't know why. They drank and took meth. His joy was genuine and categorical, and he danced with one of the girls, acting silly, playing the fool, until he felt her hands on his crotch as he turned. Ten fingers like ten bony, black twigs on his zipper. She wasn't all that ugly, he thought. She had very thin lips with reddish, almost ocher-colored lipstick and round, brown, childlike eyes. Her tan stopped abruptly, and a white shadow glowed on her shoulder. Which one was she? Frani? Duli? Moni? By that stage, he was too embarrassed to ask.

"So, I guess this means you're happy to see me," she joked.

"Yes."

Thirty minutes later they were a quarter of a mile from the fair, off in the dunes, in the dark. The sand made their steps clumsy, like those of two astronauts abandoned on a dark planet. The girl's saliva had a strong, fruity taste, as though she'd been drinking perfume; he worried that his near-total lack of experience would be obvious. Each time he kissed her, he felt both excited and a little bit disgusted; her tongue was rough and much larger than her tiny mouth would ever have led him to suspect. When he took off her T-shirt, he saw the whiteness of her two pitiful little breasts, a pair of crosscut lemons with pointy black nipples on top and three hairs sticking out. He licked them. She broke into a fit of laughter. The air looked full of tiny, floating particles. It struck him that she was ashamed of those hairs, and her shame was the one thing about her that moved him that night, perhaps because it was the one thing they had in common. The sea glimmered in the distance, a grayish light, and from time to time the crashing of waves could be heard, like crackling plastic followed by a whispery effervescence. He thought he could summon up his courage now, he could say it now. He leaned closer, but on doing so felt like his face gave him away, like without intending to, he looked somehow pathetic. *How can she even like me?* he wondered in shock. And then, almost by accident, he said it.

"Will you suck my dick?"

Her face was like a bright landscape suddenly darkened by the shadow of a lone cloud. She went very serious, tugged her shirt back down.

"I liked you better before," she said, doing up her bra beneath her T-shirt.

And then, after a silence, "I'll do you if you do me first."

"Do what?"

"Are you an idiot or do you just act like it?"

Curiosity curbed shame and disgust. His almost complete ignorance of what was before him, right there and then, aroused a strange, biological urge as he watched her sit on the trunk of a pine tree, pull up her miniskirt, and remove her panties. He could hardly see a thing in the murky shadows of the dunes until she was very close, and then the sight of her *thing* transfixed him. She had a mole on a fold of skin by her crotch, and her hair was waxed into what looked like Nefertiti's crown, and there was a small tattoo there—a star.

"Is that a tattoo?" he asked, as though striking up a friendly conversation, as though it were a baby in a crib and he were inquiring *boy or girl?*

"Yes, it's a tattoo."

She sounded annoyed, so he decided not to ask anything else. He put his tongue on her *thing*. He brushed it with pursed lips, not knowing how exactly to move, or not move, and the smell and taste were too new for him to know whether he liked or disliked it. He was leaning toward dislike, but wavering, as though sampling an expensive delicacy for the first time, one that some relative had brought from a far-off land where everyone thought it was just *exquisite*. He was enthralled, though more by the contemplation of her leg muscles tensing, her buttocks clenching, each movement of his lips and tongue producing an immediate response in a body part whose workings he couldn't quite comprehend, yet could in some way intuit. After a few seconds, he felt as though he were conducting a science experiment—felt curious rather than excited, almost—but then suddenly, from one moment to the next, the girl clenched his head between her thighs and pulled his hair, gave a little shriek and then quickly pushed his head away.

"Did I hurt you?"

She gaped at him, as though she couldn't believe what she was hearing, then burst out laughing.

"What *planet* are you from?" she asked, putting her panties back on, still giggling.

A variety of emotions danced around him like grainy light, like something with different degrees all functioning independently. Humiliation was one of them. He felt as though he'd been submerged in something viscous and was now weak and defenseless, although his initial feeling was still one of incredulity.

"Now it's your turn," he said.

"Might help if you took your pants off, don't you think? And your underwear . . ."

So he did, and turned around again just in time to catch sight of her running back toward the bright lights of the fair, twisting around every three steps to check and see if he was following or not. He didn't even bother trying to chase after her. He just turned back to the beach and slowly pulled up his underwear, and then his pants.

Humiliation, though, had its own particular prosody. What had first been expressed as incredulity soon turned to vexation. His mouth was still sticky from her *thing*, he was still dazed, and the booze and meth had left him in a heightened state of sensitivity, and cold. It was a state that made him feel as though everyone around him were possessed, filled with strange desires, dancing frantically, whirling like tops, having visions. He walked back to the fair. Pablo, Marcos, Tejas, and Rivero had disappeared with the girls, but he saw the kids from the club. They were all clustered in a little group by one of the rides. It was the first time he'd seen them all summer. He saw himself as older than them, and them as identical to the previous summer—blond or almost blond, well-dressed, pretty girls and good-looking boys—he saw them as frozen, timeless. They recognized him. He walked over. For nearly half an hour he forgot about what had just happened in the dunes. No one attempted conversation with him; they kept talking amongst themselves, and he adopted the reclusive and slightly timorous role he'd played the previous summer, like someone trying on an old costume and finding that it still fits.

It all started when one of the boys—a stocky kid, stronger than him, whose name he couldn't even recall—snorted and said, "I have to take a piss, I'm about to bust."

And he turned toward the pine trees and stumbled clumsily off.

"Wait up," he said, "I'll go with you."

They walked fifty or so feet past the rides and started pissing against a tree, in silence. Suddenly he felt a strange rage surge up.

"You know what? I've always thought you were assholes. You and the others."

The boy stood with a smile frozen on his face as he turned to face him, doing up his zipper. He looked fairly drunk but also totally sure of himself. Tomás despised with all his might the cockiness and stupidity that kid seemed to ooze.

"Then we're even," he said calmly, "'cause I've always thought you were an asshole, too."

They were silent a moment. He didn't think he had it in him to really lose his shit, but the kid kept goading him.

"So, what? You going to hit me or what?"

Almost before the kid finished the question, he leapt, trying to punch him in the face, but all he did was cuff his ear. The kid socked him, hard, in the mouth, and he found himself on the ground beside him, feeling like something in his chest was writhing, feeling fragments of things—plans, expectations, anxieties—all chopped up into tiny pieces like shards of glass, dislodging inside him and suddenly making him insecure and vulnerable, the voltage of that fight and the increasingly clear conviction that he was going to lose it. He managed to punch him again, but there was no conviction behind it, and that was what finally unleashed the boy's fury; he immediately struck back so hard that Tomás almost lost consciousness, and by the time he recovered, the kid was on top of him, gripping his wrists, trembling. He felt—and not for the first time—a strange urge to take a real beating, to be buried by blows, by the fury of another, as though secretly believing that if that were to happen, the world around him would change, everything would be transformed, become something else. Seen from below, the boy's face was almost monster-like.

"So, what should I do now, asshole? Kill you, or what? Huh, asshole? Should I kill you? What should I do with you?"

Later, standing at the bathroom mirror, before going to bed, he pulled out his cell phone and took a picture of himself. When he got into bed, trying not to make any noise, so as not to wake anyone, he looked at the photo, the light from his phone faintly illuminating the dark room—his face, split lip, eyes open, deranged as a starving animal.

It would happen in the summer, in certain places, at certain times. He and Anita were close, the two of them formed their own private community, one inexistent in the wintertime; though perhaps that was an excuse, to say that it was summer and since it was summer it was acceptable. He would turn to her and suddenly become aware of her admiration—a gaze so steady he got the feeling that his face was being engulfed by hers, even though hers was smaller. He was inside of her, like some farfetched, make-believe character, and when they walked from the house to the beach, he'd slip her his hand, pretending to have done it unawares, and Anita would say nothing, and that was the way they expressed their love. Inexplicably, at those moments, it was as if they were protecting each other from anything unpleasant, as if he threw her something, or she him, and their contact were mitigating the heat, the hot sand on the beach, their parents' rankling concern ("What do you mean, you fell? How? You left the fair and you fell, just like that?"—Mamá) and tensions and desires; she seemed to lean tenderly and affectionately into him as she walked slightly ahead, as though she wanted them to bump into each other the whole time, and it made him feel an almost violent tenderness for her—her tiny size, her round little legs, her miniature chest and features were a child-size consolation. Later, at the snack bar on the beach, his father said, "Tell me the truth, who did you get in a fight with yesterday?"

"No one, I fell."

"Right, and when you fell, the only things that hit the ground were the knuckles on your right hand, and your lip?"

He couldn't help but smile. His father gave him a light, affectionate cuff on the back of the neck. He felt very adult.

"Was it worth it, at least?"

"What?"

"Whatever you fought over."

"No."

"It's never worth it, son."

And suddenly he seemed weak to him. There was a brief silence. He was pleased with the intimacy they'd established but deep down hoped desperately that it would end there, that his father wouldn't ask anything else. And he didn't, because he was in fact thinking about something else and had been absent throughout the entire conversation.

"Your aunt is very sick," he said. "She's dying."

His father looked up from his beer and stared at him fixedly.

"We're going to bring her back to Madrid with us; I don't want her to be alone."

But there was no need to bring her back to Madrid; she was admitted to the hospital the very next day. She'd gotten some test results back, and the doctor insisted that she be admitted *immediately*. His parents got a call on their cell phone while they were at the beach, and they went straight to the hospital without so much as stopping home to change first. He was struck by an absurd thought: *They're going to get everything all sandy, they'll go into her room and get it sandy, and the hospital room will get all gross, and Aunt Eli's bed will get sandy; sand will get everywhere.* Perhaps it was easier to think about sand than death, or Aunt Eli, even. Because if sick-Aunt-Eli was still a decontextualized concept—something almost abstract, distended by incredulity despite the fact that he'd watched her deteriorate that summer—then deathbed-Aunt-Eli was a flat-out fiction, like a room with no joists, one that was impossible to enter. He felt a weird harshness in the air, almost like being hit by something inhuman. They sent him to Aunt Eli's, to get sheets and toiletries and bring them to the hospital. Anita stuck by his side, and when they were on their way to her house, he told her straight-out.

"She's going to die, Anita, you know that? Aunt Eli is."

"Yes, she's going to go to heaven."

"No, not to heaven. She's just going to die. She's not going anywhere, she's going to disappear. Heaven doesn't exist."

"Yes it does."

"No—*it doesn't.*"

Anita fell silent then. He had to force himself not to walk at his normal speed, so she wouldn't have to run to keep up. Anita frowned a little, as though attempting to destroy something inside her and then giving up.

"Yes."

"NO."

Anita was an unusual little girl. Sometimes she seemed cold, as though she'd learned from the time she was a baby to absorb things without touching them at all, to go unnoticed, moving from place to place on her tiny little legs, with her birdlike expression; other times she seemed very different, moved to an almost insufferable degree by other people's pain, and that was when she walked the way she was walking now, as though dragging something behind her, something heavy and dense and hazardous. The house smelled of talc and cheap food, like Aunt Eli. Anita cowered behind him.

"Does the house scare you?"

"Yes," she said, "a little."

Her candor was directly proportional to her fear. Later, when they were at the hospital, she seemed a thousand times braver than him. The second she walked into the room, she leapt to Aunt Eli's bedside and gave her a big, noisy smooch, and it was he who hung back in the doorway as though waiting for someone to ask if he was scared.

She looked like a corpse already, Aunt Eli did. A fat, sweaty, almost yellow corpse. He'd never realized that something as simple as a change in skin tone could foretell the imminence of someone's death with such urgency.

His father was trying to behave rationally. He made small talk, feigning upbeat confidence. Aunt Eli's replies were nonsensical.

"No matter what you say, I've always thought women were better than men."

All afternoon he acted shy and uncomfortable. When they'd been there two hours, Aunt Eli became delirious, and his father took Anita off someplace else. He stayed and watched them inject morphine, watched her face soften, watched her slowly sink into slumber looking like an obese maid who's slogged away all day and finally gets to rest but still dreams of mops and buckets. He watched her sleep there in the hospital bed, unable to recognize her and yet fascinated. He didn't feel queasy or lightheaded, he simply noted matter-of-factly the way she panted, as though the mere state of wakefulness consumed all of her energy and it could only be restored through sleep, as though that were the time for Aunt Eli's body to withdraw inward. He watched as if from afar, as if intimacy were impossible with her asleep, at a set distance, as if already standing before a corpse, or a ghost. She talked in her sleep.

"As sure as the world is round."

And fluttered a hand. Then writhed in pain. Sometimes she writhed even in her sleep. His mother started to cry. Up until that moment, he'd had a very vague idea of physical pain, and in part it was as though he'd believed it was subject to a set of rules, to certain laws. But in fact, contemplating Aunt Eli's very apparent distress, he felt as though a certain logic had been broken. He had never before suspected that life also entailed infinite shame, and that that shame was so directly and heartlessly related to physical pain. Aunt Eli was sick, and she was trapped; it was as if her pain blocked out the world, like a sickly whirlwind, impetuous, unbearably stomach-churning. Prior to that moment, pain had seemed a sort of mental state; now it was something dirty and personal, like a festering, a pointless catastrophe.

She regained consciousness briefly, for fifteen minutes or so. And said, "All this needs to be cleaned up."

And then, staring at him, she said, "Tell him that I'm right."

"Who?"

And to his father, as he walked back into the room, "I never sleep with fools, I cannot abide fools."

His father replied, a bit melodramatically, *Eli, please!*

There were six days left of summer, and Aunt Eli held on for three, during which they set up a rotation so that she was never alone and there was also always someone with Anita, who after the second day was no longer allowed back in the hospital room. Anita would ask him afterward to tell her everything he'd seen at the hospital each day, every little detail. He did the best he could and got the feeling, as he spoke, that his words were dropping down into a deep, almost bottomless pit. Anita would stare at him gravely, as though attempting to take everything in through her gaze. It seemed strange, sometimes, that this was all happening with summer at the height of its splendor. At the hospital, with his aunt, it was all so intense that her body almost seemed like a *place*. He didn't know how else to explain it—it was as if Aunt Eli's body were a place and he went *inside* it. It was sort of like making your way through an unfamiliar darkness, where you had to move in tentatively, maybe leave a trail—delicate little scraps of something—and there were echoes, and echoes of echoes, and flashes and horrifying discoveries. One of those mornings, her eyes were open, staring at the ceiling, and she wasn't saying anything, just wincing every time she felt a jolt of pain. He'd been alone with her for a while, and then an aide walked in.

"She's not speaking today."

The aide replied, "Some people are like that—the more they suffer, the less they complain. They just lie there with their eyes open, silent."

When she left, after cleaning the room, he took out his cell phone and, holding it at very close range, took a picture of Aunt Eli. It was a bizarre picture. Her eyes were open, staring straight at him. Her hair was messy, her lips slack and swollen from the pain, and in the photo there was a softness to her skin—which was covered in purplish spots—that her real face did not possess; it was as if some milky substance had oozed from the phone's tiny screen, filming her over. But what frightened him most about the picture was that there didn't seem to be anything there to look at. Aunt Eli pulled a hand from beneath the sheets and reached for the phone. She wanted to see that photo. They'd just administered another dose of morphine, and yet she seemed inexplicably alert.

"If anyone loved me, this is what they'd love," she said.

All of her gestures seemed real, all of her words seemed real, but there was no woman there. She had a look of sorrow on her face, but it vanished quickly, like a wet footprint left by a bare foot stepping on the shore.

"Give me a kiss," she said.

But his self-consciousness made him fearful. It wasn't the first time she'd done this. Aunt Eli was always asking to be kissed, kissed in a way he'd never kissed anyone before—not a girl, not his parents, not Anita. And he couldn't kiss her that way, nor did he.

He saw them for the second time on one of the afternoons he was watching Anita while his parents were at the hospital—the girls. They were always in the same place, on the shore where he'd first met them four days ago with Marcos, Pablo, Tejas, and Rivero. Perhaps they did it to be more easily found, or maybe they actually liked it there, though that was hard to believe. He was with Anita at an outdoor café that looked out over the estuary; they'd each ordered an *horchata* with the ten euros his father had given them to treat themselves to something. They didn't know what to do with themselves those afternoons and wandered around like a couple of adults diagnosed with heart conditions—begrudgingly, and only because the doctor had prescribed it. He recognized Duli—or Moni, or Frani, or whatever the name of the dune girl was—and she seemed to recognize him. They stared at one another for thirty seconds, until he finally looked away. Involuntarily, he blushed. There was a new girl with them this time. From a distance she looked slightly older, or bigger boned, but her movements were more childlike and uncoordinated. It took him nearly ten minutes to realize she was retarded. They were playing with her—badgering her, really—until she got worked up, and then they'd leave her be, and then five minutes later they'd get her all worked up again. She let out high-pitched squeals, and from where they were, it was impossible to tell if she were capable of any other form of expression. At one point they put an enormous floatie around her and all went into the water together, which excited her to what seemed a near-painful frenzy. He watched everything, down to her attempts to breathe. Duli or Moni or Frani kept turning back every three seconds to make sure he was still watching, but it was that girl and not her that he was really looking at. She looked like she was swimming through the world. There wasn't a single beautiful thing about her, not even her delight. In fact, her delight may have been the thing that seemed most deranged. It deformed her face hideously, in precisely the same way a normal person's face would be deformed by disconsolate sobbing, or hearing insufferable screeching. But she was delighted. The intensity of it couldn't possibly last. And indeed, within a few minutes it seemed to morph into something unpleasant to both herself and the other girls, and they pulled her from the water and dried her with a towel, and she simply stood there and let them. Then she plopped, exhausted, onto the sand.

"Do you know those girls?" Anita asked.

"No. Well, yeah, one of them."

The girls huddled in a little circle, colluded, told the retarded girl something or other, and then a second later they all turned toward him, openly gaping. He felt a jolt of mortification and looked away.

"They're pointing at you," Anita said.

When he turned back, the retarded girl was headed for their table, still out of breath from her swim, legs still sandy; the others hung back and watched closely. She made it to where they sat and planted herself before them. From up close, she looked almost like some kind of make-believe creature—a naiad, a semi-amphibious being. Her back was too beefy, her head small and compressed, and her mouth took up most of her face; she had straight, shoulder-length hair, plastered to her skull, two thick-set legs, and hips as wide and powerful as a mare's haunches. She even looked rough to the touch. The only thing that seemed truly alive were her eyes and hands, which had a life of their own, moving independently from the other parts of her body, although she didn't seem capable of perceiving that disconnect. From the outside, she gave the impression that on the inside, her brain was full of warm tunnels, all pulsating and palpitating, and that within them something ordinary and yet simultaneously unimaginable was taking place, as if reality had splintered into tiny shards within her.

She'd exploded into the café so recklessly that, without meaning to, she crashed into a woman, inciting great expectancy. Everyone stared with a compassionate sort of exasperation. She turned to the other girls and shouted from right where she stood.

"Thiiiiiiiis one?"

He saw her point to him and began to sweat profusely. The girls said yes from off in the distance. Then she turned back to him, as though she'd known him all his life, joyful as a dog who's just found the stick he was thrown.

"Frani says she had fun the other day and you should meet up again if you want and she owes you something."

Her voice was unbelievably nasal, and since she'd just run all the way from the shore, she was panting, too. A vein in her neck throbbed. The entire café had turned to watch. Twenty or so people with nothing to do, as was always the case with the people in that café, forever waiting for something of interest to occur on the esplanade. And here he was, handing it to them on a silver platter—he was choice entertainment, and they had front-row seats. They smirked hatefully and would recount everything they'd seen the minute they got home, in the protracted way that made banal events take on great significance only in the summer.

She was awaiting his reply.

"Tell Frani we'll see, another day," he replied.

The girl shot out like a flash, as though his words themselves had now become the stick, and the stick were flying through the air several yards ahead of her, toward the girls. She had a grimly comical way of running, as though trying to restrain herself a little. It was as if she'd been told repeatedly not to run like that and were trying not to but having no success— or having success only when she remembered, because she did it jerkily. Each step slapped noisily against the esplanade's white tiles.

Humiliated, he took advantage of her exit to pay as quickly as possible and snatched Anita up by the hand, yanking her almost airborne from the café.

"I don't want to go," Anita complained.

"Well, *I do.*"

He wanted to flee as quickly as possible and forced himself not to look back at the girls again, but before they'd made it even ten yards down the walk, toward the house, he heard the aggressive sound of her footfalls slapping behind him once more.

"Look, she's coming back," Anita said.

He turned and once again found her before him, breathing heavily. On her face, exhaustion had a cruel and uncouth quality to it.

"Frani says when's another day and to tell her when another day is so she knows when."

She was almost out of breath. Her insistence struck him as odd, as though she were trying to make some linguistic subtlety clear to a person who barely speaks the language, but there was no way to avoid it, those were the rules of the game. The girl herself seemed part of the game, as well, an inconceivable messenger huffing and puffing pitifully, in exhaustion, eyes bright with expectation because he was about to tell her something that she would then have to relay to someone else, and she looked so devoted, so capable of carrying on like that ad infinitum, that for a second he forgot the mortification that had caused him to leap up and rush from the café. How old was she? Fifteen? Twenty? Twenty thousand years old?

"Tell Frani I don't know; my aunt is dying, I have to go to the hospital every day."

He said *my aunt is dying* as though saying *the world is going to end in two hours, what does it matter if you and I see each other?* The girl stood stock still then, and the involuntary smile that excitement had plastered on her face fizzled strangely, as though being rolled up.

"Your aunt. Poor thing," she said.

"Yeah, poor thing."

When she ran off this time, she did it even faster and more earnestly. And she was no longer worried about trying to run at all attractively. Her bathing suit had crept up her butt, and she made no attempt to pull it out; it was as though she were no longer concerned about her body being exposed to the curiosity of others.

At the hospital with Aunt Eli, when he closed his eyes, he pictured Frani sucking his dick. They were back in the dunes, and all he could see was the top of her head, moving evenly, rhythmically, bobbing like a set of waves. The image bristled with impatience, full of tiny, violent particles, elusive and abstract, he pictured something like a slide, lined with silky, smooth animal fur, bathed in a silvery light; sometimes the image was crisp, but a strange noise was all it took for it to vanish, and there were constantly strange noises. Dark images overlapped. What could they possibly know about Aunt Eli's desires, or her pain? Each of them felt a bit humiliated in her presence, even his father.

"What are you thinking about?" his mother asked one time as they were walking out of the room.

And his father replied crisply, "I was thinking what a fool I am."

"Why would you say something like that?"

"I don't know."

And yet each morning and evening with delirious-Aunt-Eli followed a very similar pattern, one they'd only be able to make sense of much later. First she went into a state akin to fear, defiance. She'd always been prone to hyperbole, even when her emotions were genuine.

"I still love you; it's pathetic, but I still love you," she said, staring at his father.

"But—what did I ever do to you?"

"What did you do to me? You were ashamed of me. You abandoned me in this piece-of-shit town, that's what you did. I want it to hurt you as much as it does me."

Then would come remorse, and she'd fall silent. Pulling her hand from beneath the sheets (it was queasy-making, the way she had a constant chill despite the heat), she would reach out to him. His father would immediately take her hand, hurt, his face red as a just-fired brick, and for a few minutes it was as if through their hands, their contact, everything she'd just said was washed away, or perhaps one thing mysteriously compensated for the other. Her father would ask something banal.

"Do you like looking out the window? Would you like us to ask if your bed can be moved over by the window?"

And she'd say yes. The three of them moved her bed to the window, and then the next phase seemed to set in, a phase in which Aunt Eli would start to forget things. She closed her eyes, and he got the feeling her brain had become some sort of dark, silent theater—that what her brain thought and what her senses felt were one single, indistinguishable thing.

On the third afternoon, when she died, it was like she'd just gone to sleep, like the other times. It took them twenty minutes to realize she was dead. He often thought about that later, that they'd been by her side for twenty minutes, tending to her as though she were alive. They'd spent twenty minutes tending to a corpse.

The warmth of the sun, the faint whisper of waves they could hear from the balcony of their rental house—all of it had become sort of removed. All that afternoon, he felt as if the four of them had turned into some wide-open, gaping *thing*, as if despite the fact that they didn't part company for the rest of the whole day, they were no longer a unit, as if each of them had become aware of their own skin and their own name and it couldn't be shared with the others, as if there were a plaster wall between them. When they addressed one another, their words, too, hung haltingly in the air. The darkening of their voices, the sudden remoteness of everything, the conviction that *that* was what death was, or at least how death began, made even their movements seem sluggish, solemn.

There were lots of things to be done, but he told his father he wanted to go for a walk. He texted Rivero, and then Tejas. They were at the dock. He'd have liked to think he was going to confide in his friends, but he knew they weren't his friends and he didn't even plan to tell them. There were only three days left of summer. Suddenly, it occurred to him that his pride could only be salvaged if he didn't mention anything about Aunt Eli. Before leaving the house, he locked himself in the bathroom and tried to cry, but he couldn't. He felt full, and enthralled by his own strange self-awareness, as though he were on the verge of making a discovery and in order to do it had to avoid conventional responses and wait, attentive.

Pablo, Marcos, Tejas, and Rivero had changed a little, too, or at least that's how it suddenly seemed to him when he saw them on the dock. They struck him as subtler, shrewder, more somber. Up until then he'd felt conscious of the limits of their intelligence; now, in a way, he saw himself as less intelligent than them—diminished, somehow. Rivero's beauty and strength struck him as near mythological.

"Where you been, princess? Haven't seen hide nor hair of you for five days."

"At the hospital."

Now they'd ask him, he thought, and what could he say?

"Why?"

"My aunt, she died this afternoon."

Tejas spat.

"Well, well, well," said Pablo.

"His father died, too, two months ago—had a bad trip," Rivero said, pointing to Marcos. "The guy was a bastard."

"He was always a bastard. Now he's a dead bastard," Tejas remarked.

Marcos didn't say a word. He sat down and stared at the dock, as though he were authorizing the conversation but didn't want to encourage it. In a way, it was as if from within the habitually serious and inexpressive person that Marcos was, there had materialized an ordinary, easily wounded, delicate boy.

"They found him in the estuary. He must have gotten wasted, and the tide dragged him out and then brought him back to shore over by the breakwater, by the sea."

"No one wanted him, not even the sea," Tejas said.

Marcos smiled.

He spent a few more hours with them that afternoon, and although they didn't bring it up again, he had a strange feeling, as if their eyes had turned sort of yellow, green, white, shiny— like the pines and the dunes. They seemed to have a hard, ironic look he'd never, until that moment, noticed—or perhaps he just hadn't understood it, because he was so blindingly naïve. He liked the way they conceptualized and experienced death, which was actually hardly any different from the way they experienced and conceptualized sex. Death was absolute negation with no privileges. You could skirt death, describe its shape, weigh it in the palm of your hand, long for it or fear it, but you couldn't find any logic to it. Just as they had no notion of the future, Pablo, Marcos, Tejas, and Rivero had no notion of anything distant. They were the princes of that rundown town that came to life only in summer; they were already, in their adolescent way, real men—wary, macho, triumphant. All four of them seemed almost the embodiment of an oft-imagined older brother, one who'd experienced many of the darker sides of life and yet was nearly always friendly and optimistic anyway. With them by his side, he didn't feel deceived. They walked toward the beach, and as they sauntered down the esplanade, he hoped someone was watching, admiring, perhaps spying on all five of them through a little hole, or that someone was thinking *Hate to bump into those guys in a dark alley at night.*

And in fact someone was watching them through a little hole. He saw her coming toward them in the distance but didn't realize who it was until she got right up close. It was the retarded girl who'd been with the others at the estuary—the messenger with her little stick. She was alone, walking along in a bikini, legs all sandy, a huge floatie ring under her arm, still inflated. He felt ashamed, as if the girl knew something private or had witnessed some barely memorable event that had then been recounted down to the most excruciating detail. She stopped in front of them.

"Where you going, Marita?"

"Home," she replied, staring only at him.

"You know each other?" Rivero asked.

"That's Frani's boyfriend," she explained, pointing at him.

"Right, in Frani's dreams." (Tejas)

"Frani says the other day he ate her pussy in the dunes, and that's a boyfriend," she explained, with the staggering candor and calm air of someone in possession of irrefutable evidence. It was as if the words that came out of her lips had been other, entirely acceptable words, everyday words. And as she spoke them, she eyed him triumphantly, defying him to have the guts to deny it.

"Who'd have thought—the princess!"

"What about you, Marita? How many boyfriends have you had this summer?"

"Two."

"Good ones or bad ones?"

"One good, one bad."

"What about us?" Rivero asked.

"You're bad," she replied solemnly.

Then they watched her disappear toward the boxy houses at the end of the estuary. She walked with great dignity, with such a desire to be liked, such flair—like an actress on the red carpet on opening night.

"Would you look at that?" Tejas said. "That girl likes sucking dick more than most people like sucking on shrimp."

"Till someone gets her pregnant. Then all hell's going to break loose."

"Out of the depths I have cried unto Thee, oh Lord. Lord, hear my voice; let thy ears attend my cry. If Thou should mark iniquities, oh Lord, who could then draw near? But forgiveness is thy way, that Thou may be respected."

If he turned just slightly to the left, he could see everyone; there were only ten people in total: his parents, Anita, and Aunt Eli's four or five friends. The overall impression it gave was sterile, tragic. They'd been forced to go out that morning to buy clothes, since all they'd packed were beach clothes—bathing suits and T-shirts. And the act of having to buy clothes, even, was irritating. The few shops in town had nothing remotely resembling mourning attire, and as a result they all ended up in white, or pastel tones, looking like little more than affluent holidaymakers.

"We'll dress in white. If we can't dress for mourning, we'll dress in white; Aunt Eli would have liked that." (Mamá)

"It'll look like we're going to a wedding." (Papá)

And it did. Anita couldn't sleep at all that night. She had dreamed about Aunt Eli and come to his bed, woken him up.

"I can't sleep. I'm scared."

"What are you scared of?"

"Aunt Eli."

Her arms were like very thin cotton, hanging lifelessly on either side of a white dress she'd probably never wear again, because, despite her age, Anita had already developed an inexplicably precise set of superstitions. His father requested they open the coffin one last time as Aunt Eli was taken from the funeral home, and her face appeared—all of them gathered around as though staring down into a well—Aunt Eli's face there like a fat sunflower, pale and spongy. He thought then, for the first time, *This is real; she's dead.*

The coffin was pretty, lacquered in creamy brown, like a giant bonbon. As it was lowered from the hearse, everyone crowded around to help, though it turned out not to be necessary, both because it was on wheels and because the hearse drivers themselves carried it to the nave inside the cemetery's small church. They worked with such efficiency, using such a strange device—with little, fold-down wheels—that for a few seconds everyone was more mesmerized by the men and what they were doing than by the coffin.

As the deer thirsts for water, Lord, so my soul longs after Thee. My soul thirsts after the living God. When shall I come and appear before God? He could detect the vibration of each word, but he'd been stripped of emotion. It had started yesterday. A feeling he got the sense only Anita shared. During the funeral procession, in the car on the way to the cemetery, he gave Anita his hand. The front row of the funeral party had an introspective and slightly anarchic air, while the back row, where Aunt Eli's friends were, showed more of a sense of imposed solemnity. The priest walked behind the coffin wearing a professional expression. The cemetery opened out on both sides and everyone was glancing around at the graves a bit distractedly. He could see himself watching, see himself there among all those props as though backstage, on a set. He watched himself, as if he were experiencing Aunt Eli's death, as if the death of Aunt Eli were real and true one second and then so fake the next that she required the whole ridiculous performance they were putting on, and then true once more, but with no real emotion behind it. It was as if someone who didn't belong had just burst in and interrupted a dance, and they'd all stopped and were waiting for somebody else to come and explain the reason for the interruption, but no one did, and the dance simply ended, and that was it. That was the way the dance ended.

"We deliver you, dear sister Eli, to almighty God, we deliver you unto Him who created you, that you may return to God, who formed you from the dust of the earth."

The wreaths were brought out and laid on top of the coffin, but they wouldn't fit in the grave and had to be smashed down a little, thereby immediately losing all their dignity. The grave looked, now, like some sort of landfill for flowers.

"Now that your soul has left your body, may the splendid hierarchy of angels come to greet it; may the noble army of martyrs, the triumphant band of confessors attend around you; may the jubilant chorus of virgins hail you; and may you be held fast in the blessings of peace, in the bosom of the patriarchs. May you be a stranger to all that is punished with darkness, with flames, and condemned to torments. May none of the ministers of Satan dare to stop you in your way. May he tremble in your approach in the company of angels. May he with confusion fly away into the vast chaos of the night. Amen."

"Amen," they echoed.

The first to throw a handful of dirt was Anita, at Mamá's urging. Next came his father, his mother, Aunt Eli's friends, and it was then— when everyone turned to him, to let him through, as he crouched to take a handful from the little mound beside the grave and was about to walk up to the pit—that he felt for the first time since she'd died as if Aunt Eli's life were flowing solemnly and somberly over them, above their heads, as if she were vanishing into the cemetery air and coiling around the trees, somehow obscured, and as if surprised at herself, or disconnected, like a landscape that by dint of being observed, is transformed. He thought, *Here it comes, now I am going to feel sorrow,* and he stood quietly, attentive. But sorrow did not come. What came was rage.

He remembered his hands, the feeling his hands produced all afternoon as he packed his bags in silence in a house he'd never again live in, and the abrasive, aching sound of the dunes from the balcony, and the faint, downy contact of his mother's cheek when she came into his room to give him a kiss. And the day almost seemed to refuse to end—the afternoon went on and on with its vertical, white light. It was white grief, bleak by virtue of its sheer light, and now it opened its big, soft doors. White was the color of death. They hardly spoke all day. In a way, it was as though they had already gone back to living their winter lives, weighed down by obligations, and each of them carried the private burden of their individual problems—problems that go unshared, because they're trivial, but are still the stuff of everyday existence. Secreted behind closed lips were all the things they'd felt and only very timidly dared to share. Their way of dealing with Aunt Eli's death said this, that they belonged to one another, that they were alike, but also alone.

That was when he first got the feeling, as he was packing his suitcase. Initially like a vague sort of irritation, one with no real object, and then cold, full of genuine rage—they'd deceived him. Not his parents specifically—all of them. He'd been deceived. He raised a hand and held it out before him; he'd been staring at the thought like a lunatic. Sometimes he felt ashamed not to have seen it sooner. But what was it that he'd seen, exactly? He didn't know . . . the deceit. A sort of wind that swept over everything, brushing it all into a corner of the world. He felt a strange urge to be violent, impetuous, voracious, as if something were about to rise up from those effulgent dunes and swallow everything, even him, the way it had Aunt Eli. Summer was over. The next day they'd take the train home, and he'd be back in the city. Was that how it was all going to end? It couldn't end like that. He texted, *Leaving tomorrow meet up tonight*, and sent it to Rivero. On his cell phone's tiny screen, a miniature envelope sealed itself and darted off. Message sent. And ten seconds later, *Sure, princess.* He felt like getting drunk, and high, like something had grabbed him by one arm and roughly thrust him forward. The way his parents expressed their grief got on his nerves for the next three hours until he went out; it was both mawkish and cautious, an emotion half expressed and half restrained, as though they were horrified at the thought of perhaps being too explicit. His father wept alone for a time, on the balcony, and he watched his back, contracting in rhythmic little spasms, from his bedroom window. Even without seeing his face, he could see the way his lips were turning down, the way his nose was running, the way he was staring off at the dunes—with the same stunned look he'd had at the cemetery— and spilling something soft and warm over them. His own state of mind made him no less uneasy. He saw himself as cold, as though he'd been injected with a virus that inhibited emotional reaction. Actually, he felt nothing, and not feeling anything was a state in and of itself, an uneasiness perceived precisely due to its absence. He remembered it as if something had, for those three hours, been growing—a disposition perhaps—as if something inside him had flipped a lever that enabled certain things to occur, things up to that point only imagined. He remembered, too, that during the course of those hours he felt open contempt for the naïveté with which he'd lived his life up until then and that he sensed what would later turn into the cold courage (because, ironically, the experience of courage was a cold one) of someone determined to be intransigent. He was fascinated by the sentiment; it floated like a soft mist as the afternoon faded away, and it penetrated him—spent—the way Aunt Eli's dead face had penetrated him when they opened her casket on the way out of the funeral home.

"But—you're not going out, are you?" (Mamá)

"Yes."

"Oh, how *could* you?"

He still had childlike reactions; suddenly he was afraid he wouldn't be allowed.

"Just for a little while."

"Let him go, let him do what he wants." (Papá)

And when he got outside, the feeling intensified; the esplanade with its huge, white tiles was a giant skating rink. Anita had accompanied him to the door and asked if she could come too. Without a word, he'd pushed her out of the way, as if she were some bothersome angel who'd approached him extending a gentle, knowing arm.

"At least tell me where you're going."

"Move."

When he met up with them, it was already dark, and since it was a Saturday, the bars were packed. All along the esplanade, sidewalk cafés and snack bars formed a refulgent wake, as though a luminous ship, tall and elegant, had sailed through town from one end to the other, as though the houses were actually aquatic, enormous buoys bobbing in the water.

"A kid drowned here last summer," Rivero said.

They hadn't even smartened up to go out. He had, and therefore looked slightly ridiculous, as if it were his first communion and he were still dressed as a little sailor when everyone else had already changed into more comfortable clothes. The comment precluded most all conversation, so no one said anything.

"So you're leaving tomorrow?"

"Yeah, tomorrow."

"We'll have to give you a proper sendoff."

"No need."

"Oh, we have to have a sendoff for the princess who wanted to break our noses with a rock."

They laughed. In other circumstances he might have felt obliged to smile, a little humiliated, maybe. Deep down, he'd been so trained to please, to be liked by everyone, that fear of not being liked was the one thing that had most notably formed his character. He saw, now, that almost everything he'd done his whole life he'd done specifically to be liked, or for fear of not being liked, and that that had now changed. Since Aunt Eli died, he'd had not a single purely considerate thought—not even about himself, and certainly not about Pablo, Marcos, Tejas, and Rivero. In fact, he felt like he held them in contempt a little now, or like his rage had slid a sort of film of discontent, or violence, between them and him.

They bought a few bottles of booze at a Chinese corner store and sat by the estuary. They took the meth Tejas had brought. The violence actually began there, timidly, like a blood transfusion from his veins to theirs. The alcohol and the meth interfered with one another, throwing things into and out of balance, but he didn't feel heavy, he felt instead cold and lucid, like a hunter polishing the barrel of his gun with controlled intoxication.

"What about Frani? Aren't you going to say goodbye to her?"

"Leave him alone, man. Can't you see he's a total virgin? Like a five-year-old. For now all he does is eat pussy. Frani wouldn't know where to start with this kid."

It was working. A sort of fervor was being roused in them, too; they, too, were caught in its talons. They were no longer sitting as they talked by the estuary but had stood, restless; the meth had worked its mysterious effects and now hit them, rising like liquid in a test tube held over a flame. Icy, blue liquid. Marcos threw a bottle into the water and picked up another.

"See that boat there?"

And he threw it, hard. The bottle shattered against the hull.

"You couldn't do that again if you tried."

"But that's going to end tonight," he suddenly blurted.

His response had been a bit delayed. It had traveled the entire length of his nerves, his stomach, his brain. More than an idea or even a response, it was a messianic vision on a night moving inexorably forward, its minutes dropping off into the darkness. It was going to end that very night.

"What's going to end?"

"I'm going to fuck tonight."

"Frani?"

"Or whoever."

It was like standing majestically before an army that was whipping itself into a frenzy. He needed a little death, a little nobility around him, something to attest to the grandiosity of the idea, something to keep him from being alone with it. The idea suddenly overrode all other sensations. For a few minutes it wasn't even attached to the desire to have sex, but to possess or explode. Its slightly hazy contours, slowly sharpening into a concrete image, made it even grander, *more* powerful if anything, as though his mind were crowded with hundreds of bodies floating blindly, uncontrollable.

"We'll have to go find the girls." (Pablo)

"They were outside at that café, I think."

"Let's go."

The distance between the boys and their destination was covered in silence. Determination had dripped down inside them. The town's physical reality, too, had become altered. He looked around, and it was as if all the people sitting at outdoor bars and cafés, all the people strolling along the esplanade and moving behind well-lit windows were possessed by that same sentiment, too; they were servile, tormented by it, no matter what they said, whether the poses they struck were more restrained or less, they were all possessed by the same nervous impatience. When he turned back to them, he got, for the first time, the strange feeling that he was their leader, as if his body were channeling their fury. Marcos laughed nervously, and Rivero put a hand on his shoulder. Rivero's hand, like a taut cable.

But the girls weren't there. Nor were they at the other outdoor café they often hung out at.

"Where are those tramps?"

"They must be somewhere."

Hunger was snapping at their heels. They spent an hour searching for them, flummoxed. They tried, with no luck, to pick up another group of girls at a café and very nearly caused a fight at a bar they ended up getting kicked out of. Lust abated slightly in the face of reality, but not rage. Rage was still there, frozen, like a feeling superior to all others.

"Let's go back to the estuary and set a boat on fire," Pablo said.

But on their way to the estuary, they saw a shadow in the distance. An awkward shape lumbering toward them, emerging from the dark.

"No fucking way."

"What?"

"It's Marita."

Sometimes the memory begins there, in that final, softly-illuminated shadow on the esplanade, on tiles white as blocks of ice, as if there were not one dock but dozens, hundreds of rows of docks, all lined up and glazed by the electric light of the street lamps lining the way. Other times the memory begins later, when they're already heading into the dunes. Marita's feet, from behind, are clumsily large, as are her arms, their volume disproportionate to any other part of her body. She's wearing a maroon skirt and a blue T-shirt that don't match, and black flip-flops with the Brazilian flag on them. Every time she takes a step, he can see the flags on the soles of her flip-flops. She's a sullen person—not a person but a cylinder of flesh all out of proportion—and bulges out here and there as she walks. In the memory, he's behind her for a time and then he moves up beside her. Or is she the one who moves beside him? It's odd—during that space of time there is almost no sign of Marcos, Pablo, Tejas, or Rivero. And, when he looks at her, her mouth is more lusterless and rougher than it ever has been before, like a low sound in the middle of an inexpressive face. Most of the time, though, the memory is not made up of images but of sensations. The plants and branches in the memory are a tangle of dense, jungle-like vegetation that obeys a law of its own, one that has nothing to do with him. It's as if the world itself were at a critical juncture in the memory, unable to keep going, as if norms and infractions were suspended there, or had conspired to create a strange testing ground, a zero-gravity capsule. In the memory his heart is cold, like an actor in a movie who he knows doesn't have long to live.

It's strange, too—he's not sure if Marita protested right away or not; that's one thing his memory has erased completely. He doesn't know what they told her exactly, whether it was him or one of the others, what deceit set her in motion off toward the dunes. They must have spoken, there had to have been some prior conversation, some lie. But the lie, too, is missing from his memory, it's disappeared. All he knows is that Rivero, when they're walking toward the dunes, is telling Marita a story about some monkeys that escaped from the zoo, a monkey revolution, all the monkeys jumping the wall, helping one another escape, the city overrun by their screeching.

"Can you believe that?"

"Tell me again."

Marita likes having stories told to her. Later, he would search the internet, unable to find it, the implausible tale of the monkey rebellion. Rivero tells it again.

"They all escaped, can you believe it? Hundreds of monkeys jumping around, stealing kids' candy, pinching old ladies."

Marita laughs. Then comes another blank in the memory, something avoided, the leap between the end of the esplanade and the start of the dunes. And suddenly all six of them are walking through the pine trees in silence, the sound of the waves in the distance. By the time they sit down, it's all already begun. Rivero says, "Suck my dick, Marita, show these clowns how good you do it. Like the other day, remember?"

And Marita replies, "I don't want to."

In the memory, the violence doesn't begin right away. There's a lapse during which everything is still familiar and run-of-the-mill, like a trite conversation. Why does he feel like there's even a point when they laugh? Nervous laughter, like someone shaking them awake. Marita struggles a little at first, and Rivero falls onto the sand beside her. Pablo and Marcos spring to his aid, and Marita stops moving immediately.

"It's going to hurt more if you act like that," Rivero says.

He takes off her panties.

The truth is he doesn't know if that's how it goes or not. His powerlessness, the concrete, physical reality of the situation, his nervousness, it all blends together a little. In his memory he can still hear the sea in the distance, hear it at regular, rhythmic intervals, like the whiteness of Rivero's buttocks thrusting in and out between Marita's legs. She doesn't make a sound. The horror does not dissipate in the memory; it is, in fact, the only fixed image—powerless, frozen horror. The pounding of his nerves and heart is so intense it almost leaves marks on his hands, on his skin, everything seems about to meld, everything except for the bodies. Rivero gets up and Pablo crouches down. The scene is repeated. Suddenly there is a fetid, ocean smell, like rotting seaweed, a concentrated, ceremonious stench. Pablo has taken off his jeans and underwear. They're balled up on the ground beside his flip-flops, buttons glinting like fish eyes in the night. He has a hard time fixing his gaze on those two flapping bodies and instead looks a foot or two beyond them, at the reeds where Marita's panties lie. Blue panties with a nonsensical pattern. Pablo moans when he finishes, and Tejas crouches down. The operation is repeated once more, but this time it takes far longer. Marita, each time someone finishes, tugs down her skirt timidly, without moving. Tejas is on top of her now, like a stubborn child hell-bent on breaking an indestructible toy. There is a peculiar stagnation in the air, there among the pines, as Tejas raises himself up on his arms and then lets his body drop, again and again, and a fleeting sense, very faint, of the sound of flesh slapping, which lasts several minutes.

"Come on, man."

"Leave me alone, asshole."

He is still motionless, it's as if he's present but has not entirely taken shape, like a ghost who refuses to materialize. If he moves a little, turns slightly toward the beach that's visible out beyond the pine trees, the feeling becomes somewhat more pronounced, and he gazes attentively into the distance as though trying in vain to remember something, a name. If he turns back to them, the feeling reappears, but chaotic, like a simple fact, enduring, overcome, crowded by the presence of many other feelings. Tejas moans when he comes. Marcos crouches down. In the intervening moments, he sees Marita's face for a second, a millisecond. A face seemingly many miles away, a face *engulfed*. Next will come his turn; he thinks of that for the first time right then, disgusted, and the idea leaves him almost dizzy. His body had never felt that before. Fascination had never been mixed with repulsion, or sorrow, or absence. Marita gives a little shriek and says for the first time, "You're hurting me."

Rivero, Pablo, and Tejas seem a bit absent, too, now that they've finished.

"Fuck, man, don't hurt her," Rivero says.

Marcos comes immediately and climbs off, pulling up his pants. Now it's his turn. He pulls his pants down, but he's not turned on. Then, without wanting to, he does become turned on. Is it the fear? It's not, to be sure, attraction. He is turned on without meaning to be, like someone who trips without meaning to, or falls in love without meaning to. And when he gets on top of her, he feels the viscous wet of her *thing*. He decides to pretend that he's doing it. He decides to make noises, do all the things the others did, but without penetrating her. It's a snap decision, like the kind made when someone playing a game decides to cheat and all rules are suspended. Marita understands immediately and looks at him—something she didn't do with any of the others. She looks at him with eyes that are not real, as if her glance were somehow passing straight through his body and fixing attentively on something fifty feet behind him. He puts a hand on her shoulder, as though he were tired and had to use her to hold himself up, and at that instant he feels she belongs to him, pure and simple, like an object, she belongs to him. In the memory, Marita's body takes on a strange grace and fills with bones, flesh, blood, intestines. He would like to whisper something in her ear, something sweet, but he doesn't know what. He wishes he could tell her that he's sorry, that he doesn't want to be doing what he's doing, even though all he's doing is pretending. He would like to say something, anything, but he senses that her face is fading, that she can't hear him, that she isn't there, where she is. And he senses, too, in the memory, that Marita is mortal, as is he. He senses it like an ingenuous realization, one full of sentimentality. Then he pretends to come, giving two or three juddering spasms. He gets up. Marita finds her panties and pulls them on while standing, taking off her flip-flops.

"Well, that's everyone," Rivero says.

In the memory they are silent for a while, until Tejas tries to joke.

"So, princess, how's that for a sendoff?"

But no one keeps it going, not even Rivero. And the walk back along the esplanade takes longer than before. Marita walks ahead of them, more awkwardly and clumsily than usual, as though trying to get a little farther from them with each step, and then a little farther still, without their realizing, trying to get very far away. Rivero sidles up beside her.

"Marita."

"What."

"You know I've always taken care of you. You know that. Lots of times."

Marita doesn't respond.

"You know that, Marita."

A very faint *yes*.

"And you know I always mean what I say, you know that, too."

"Yes."

"If you say a word about this, I'll slit your throat. Understand? Marita, do you understand me?"

"Yes."

And then, like a spring, Marita bounds down the esplanade, as though her own *yes* were the starting gun at a race; she's running away, arms and legs flailing in a crazy dance, toward the low, boxy houses by the estuary. Marcos makes as if to follow her, but Rivero stops him immediately.

"Leave her," he says, "she won't say a word."

And in the memory it's as though after Rivero speaks, everything fades away; the esplanade by the dock, the houses lit in the yellowy light of street lamps, the sound of people still making merry at bars and cafés, the distant glimmer of the estuary, the tinkling of boats—all of it fades into a sort of faint, gray light. Does he say goodbye to them, or does he not? He doesn't even know. None of that is included in the memory; in the mishmash of things in the memory, there is even a different light, as though a new day were rising as he walked, alone, into town, and the people he passed were all very fresh-faced. Not even when he walks into the house, when his mother asks him where he's been, is he capable of speaking.

"You've been drinking," she says.

"No."

"You've been doing something—tell me what you were doing."

And she follows him to his room.

"I wasn't doing *anything*."

PART TWO
MEMORY OF OCTOBER

He would say, "Boring, like every other summer."

He would say, "One day, at the beach, I almost drowned."

He would say, "My aunt Eli died, right at the end."

The rest, he kept to himself.

He'd become a pensive young man. He had never been particularly popular in class, and that was still true at the start of the new school year. It was odd the way Madrid had the ability to absorb things, the efficiency with which everything was subsumed in the monotonous blinking of traffic lights, in the afternoon light—first white and crisp and then vaguely pastel. There seemed to be no pain or sorrow the city could not swallow, swaddling it in thin, transparent layers until it was muffled, though not gone. The city had a belly full of rocks.

His mother told them they had to help their father through this trying time. His father had become a quieter person, too, as though Aunt Eli's death had imbued him with a meekness he'd never before possessed. His health had declined a bit, and sometimes he had mood swings. Some sort of stomach trouble, a dull ache, useless and persistent, that lasted a whole month. When he wasn't in a bad mood, he became sentimental.

"I love you so much, kids," he'd say out of nowhere, in the middle of dinner, giving rise to an uncomfortable silence. He told them he loved them not as though it were a joyful proclamation or a way to erase something from the past but as though it were an ill-fated attachment, one binding them together in present and future, a way to share the road to emptiness. He himself felt a mixture of compassion and irritation; sorrow had made some of his more masculine traits dissolve.

During that first week, his own brain seemed to prevent him from thinking about what had happened. Then, from one day to the next, he got scared. He was walking down the street with Anita; it was a Sunday, and their mother had sent them down to buy the paper. The weather in the city was still balmy, and people were sitting out at sidewalk cafés. Anita was explaining to him, with surprising precision, how much she hated one of the girls in her class. They sat on a park bench, and for a minute he was unable to process what his sister was saying, he became completely self-absorbed momentarily, and then got a strange wave of vertigo. He could hear the water in the park's fountain in the distance—the sound of droplets gurgling out of the sprinkler head—and the mud encircling it, and the trees, and all the people . . . he didn't know how to explain it, it was as though suddenly they were all *too close* to one another, horrifyingly close, or imbued with something sickening. And so was he, slack and languid and viscous, and even Anita—everything slowly, senselessly rotting away. It was a type of fear he'd never before experienced, bare and perfunctory, shapeless, making him almost want to leap up from the bench where he sat and hurl himself under the first passing car. Anita asked him if he felt OK.

"You're all white," she said (Anita used only colors to describe moods: white, red, green, yellow).

"I know."

That was the first time. Over the next two weeks, it happened three more times. It wasn't the kind of fear brought on by a concrete, identifiable object, more like a state, a sort of festering of things. And there was no way to stop it from coming or even predict when it would appear. It just erupted, like sudden anguish, like some colossal finger pointing at him and making him recoil.

Little by little, he began to recall the episode with Marita, almost always at night, or when he was alone in his room doing homework. He'd start to zone out, his gaze hovering over the letters in his textbook as though dissolving them, and then her face, or something like her face, would appear there. He remembered being in the dunes, remembered the presence of Pablo, Marcos, Tejas, and Rivero. He remembered, more than anything, his own cowardice. Then came the whiteness of Rivero's ass, that ass wriggling and contracting like a slug, but not like it was on top of Marita, more like it was penetrating something fragile and delicate, a crystal glass or a little girl, and it was like he might still be there and something inside him were screaming—*What am I going to do now?* Then he'd get the jitters, a sort of dull vibration and an incessant urge to still be there so he could wrench Rivero up by the arm, shove him, punch him. It wouldn't matter if they beat the shit out of him after that—beat him and beat him and beat him. He'd get up from the chair where he'd been working and, if he was home alone, open the closet and punch the wall, and then again, in an attempt to draw blood. After the hysteria would come uneasiness and melancholy. His soul had been stretched taut as a rubber band, and then from one second to the next it was released, snapped inside. He'd say aloud, "I'm a coward."

He said *I'm a coward* not as if it were a simple description but as if it were his most essential attribute, as if it were his true nature. And when he looked in the mirror, he no longer thought *Tomás has brown hair* but *the coward has brown hair*, and if he was hungry, *the coward is hungry*, and if he was tired, *the coward is tired*.

His fourth week back was the most excruciating of all. It started with a recurrent dream—him, sitting by the seafront, back in the beach town, with Anita. They were upbeat, relaxed, and jovial, until Rivero came along. It was very hot in the dream, a muggy, unpleasant heat. It was all so real, profound, interesting; it had the same delicate quality as certain summer afternoons. Rivero's presence at first went unnoticed. Then from one second to the next, he was taking part in the conversation, too, asking Anita questions. And then suddenly he'd say, "Suck my dick, Anita."

Or maybe, "Take off your panties, Anita."

Then he'd watch him lay down on top of her, but he himself would remain motionless, right there beside them, unable to move. That was when his memory of the dream slowed inexplicably, as if Rivero and Anita were two frozen shapes, sculptures maybe, and he felt cornered, trapped, unable to reach them; the air was thick, and all he could do was crouch down beside them. He looked at Anita's face. It was the same face she'd always had, maybe a bit more inexpressive than normal, she had those tiny features he had so often adored, those little eyes, round as two coins, and her body was moving at regular, rhythmic intervals as Rivero's body slapped down on top of her. Then, suddenly, Anita's face sparked in him a kind of inexplicable revulsion. Revulsion as if something in it had vanished, or something had been poured over her. He'd wake up.

It would have been nearly impossible to explain the hysteria with which he would awake from that dream. One time he woke up screaming, which led to a small panic. He saw his mother crouching there beside him, disheveled, face puffy, smelling like sleep, eyes wide with fear.

"What on earth were you dreaming?"

He couldn't help it, he burst into tears. His mother sat down beside him and tried to hug him, but since they almost never touched, the physical contact was even more distressing. He felt like he was slipping down a soft, oily, gray hill. That was the first time he cried in front of his mother as an adult.

Rage and shame sometimes converged to form a state of full-on misery. He felt within his body the pain of things hitherto unknown— his liver, blood, stomach, lungs, heart. And disgust at the pain. And disgust at the shame. It got even worse when he found out a girl liked him. There was this one girl in his class who was kind of after him, a girl named Lourdes who had a very small body and boy's hips, who sometimes waited for him after class and didn't live far from him. She was pretty, though, her facial features had a fine, delicate beauty about them, a beauty just starting to emerge but clearly present. Her features had developed unevenly; she had full, sensual lips, but her expression was incredibly childlike and anxious, as though something inside her were teetering, constantly losing her footing on the path to becoming a woman. It wasn't specifically Lourdes' desire he found so unpleasant but desire in and of itself, any desire for bodies on top of one other. The fact that all those people—Lourdes, the other girls, men strolling past him on the street—had *done it*, or at least were always wanting to do it, imposed a kind of fatalistic quality on the world. After class, when he saw her there waiting for him, he could almost feel her desire on top of him like a slimy substance. Then, walking along beside her, Lourdes would be talking about her parents or some classmate and he couldn't help but focus on her arms, her already-developed breasts (which, curiously, she tried to squash beneath T-shirts that compressed them unnaturally), the robust, carnal message her body sent by walking so close to him. It seemed grotesque and unnecessary to use sentimental ploys to conceal something that was, in fact, grotesque and crude, and although he felt disgusted by desire, he felt equally disgusted by the fact that it couldn't be openly addressed. Lourdes would laugh, and he'd see—behind her disturbingly perfect, white teeth—a strange, repulsive tongue, a repulsive tongue darting around inside her mouth with repulsive speed, he'd see the slight trembling of her cheeks when she tried to smile, and the way the trembling persisted when she held her smile longer than necessary, and how it then became fixed, like an animal hide that's been pulled taut and laid out to dry in the sun. The quick kiss on the cheek she gave him when they got to her house and said goodbye was like a burning moth on his skin, and he would try to wear himself out when climbing the stairs, as if in need of physical exhaustion to escape the listlessness.

Only pain was real. Physical pain. Only pain had the ability to hold everything, to impose order on it, to place it within strict confines. The first time it happened, it was almost by accident. He was in bed and leaned to one side and jabbed himself with a screw sticking out of the wooden bedframe. Immediately his body flinched in pain. He touched his thigh and felt around the bed for the source. The boards on the frame's joint had separated slightly, and the tip of a long, black screw was sticking out. After that, it became a near-daily routine—he'd lie face up and inch closer to that spot until he could feel the tip of the screw in his thigh, he'd force his body not to recoil and then press firmly into it. The pain was sharp and concentrated, and his whole body tensed against it. It was as if something inside him could be at ease when he felt that pain, as if something stopped being unreal and weak. But then the pain would subside again and there would be nothing left, nothing but a round bloodstain on his pajama bottoms, which he then had to rinse out in the bathroom so no one would see.

He began to cry. It was a strange kind of crying, one sometimes brought on by the most banal of events.

"You're blue today," Anita said.

"What do you mean, blue?"

"Blue," she insisted.

"I'm not a good person, Anita, I've done very bad things."

"Me, too," she replied gravely. "If you knew . . ."

Then he'd get the feeling something was entering his body, slowly and cautiously, making his insides all soft, and then suddenly there would come a burst of anguish. The scene from the dunes would appear, startlingly sharp—sterile, monotonous, unacceptable, repetitive—he'd feel even more anxiety than he had when he was actually beside Marita, or on top of her. Then he'd go into the bathroom, get a towel, and bite down on it as hard as he could, until his jaw ached.

In early autumn he got the flu. He felt embarrassed to be taken care of, to have broth made for him, to be tucked in when he fell asleep. Anita would poke her head in from the doorway and say hello from there so as not to catch it, she would try to make him laugh and sometimes succeeded, she'd make him a drawing or come in with the laptop and they'd watch a movie together—he, lying in bed; she, sitting on the floor with a handkerchief tied over her mouth like a miniature bank robber. It was a long week of convalescence, and it happened to be the same week as his birthday. He got a black leather jacket he really liked, but as soon as he opened the package, he felt his desire recede, felt the jacket degrade to the point of seeming just a ridiculous piece of merchandise. And since the end of summer, the same thing that happened with objects he longed for had been happening with everything else; it was as if he couldn't focus his attention on them.

He spent those days at home, alone, and when his fever broke, he'd wander around the house snooping through everyone's drawers. On one of those afternoons, he discovered, in one of his father's desk drawers, the keys to Aunt Eli's house. When he touched them, it was as though he'd gotten an electric shock that ran clear through him. He picked them up and took them back to his room. He started to fantasize. The keys to Aunt Eli's house held for him the same seductive appeal every malicious object always had, like the time a boy he knew brought to class a Nazi jackknife, which he claimed had belonged to a German officer. For a few seconds he'd held that small, heavy object in his hand—it was lacquered in black with a little, white swastika on it—and felt a rush of vertigo, as if there were something evil concentrated in the object itself, or as if he couldn't touch it without being affected by its sway. Something similar happened when he brought Aunt Eli's keys back to bed with him. The keys, too, seemed to emanate some sinister power, a mysterious, irreversible pull. He hardly slept that last night he spent at home.

First came white light, then pink light, then a shadow, then white light again, pink once more, shadow; when he opened his eyes, the countryside looked frozen, even though the bus was still moving. He was having a hard time thinking clearly. It had taken a stroke of luck— an envelope containing three hundred euros he found in his parents' bedroom. He knew he didn't have much time to make up his mind about it; that money certainly wasn't going to be there for long, and he'd recovered now from the flu. The next morning, he'd left the house with his school backpack full of clothes and the three hundred euros in his pocket, but instead of heading to school, he made for the bus station. Three hours later the bus was on its way and his eyes were opening and closing. He was shocked at how easy it had all been. White light, pink light, shadow. White light, pink light, shadow. It had rained the night before, and the landscape looked both muted and shiny at the same time, as though it had been varnished and then illuminated with a very faint light.

He'd left a note saying that he'd taken the money, he had to do something important, he *had* to go away for a few days. He'd be fine. They shouldn't worry. He wrote it quickly and then thought it childish. He tore it up and wrote another, this one more succinct, apologizing and asking them to have faith in him even if they didn't understand him. He added that he'd return the money as soon as he could, he'd work to pay them back. He signed it. In a postscript, he told them not to call his cell phone—he'd left it in his room, turned off.

Aside from the escape itself, he'd made no further plans, so during the several-hour journey he tried, fruitlessly, to think about how he was going to manage once there and what it was he actually wanted to do. He regretted not having brought warmer clothes, because all he had was a couple of T-shirts and the sweater he was wearing. It had started to rain again. He wanted to see her, that was all. He wanted to see her even if it was just once and from afar, that might be enough. He didn't really know what he wanted, but for the first few hours he felt possessed by an almost violent euphoria that gradually diminished the closer the bus got to town.

It was completely dark by the time he arrived, and his mood had turned melancholy. He had a hard time almost even recognizing the place. It was the same effect as a house that's been lived in for years and then suddenly has all the furniture removed; it was all at odds somehow, smaller maybe. There was no one out on the street. It was cold.

He got scared for the first time when he realized that the electricity at Aunt Eli's house had been cut off. He didn't want to make any noise, for fear of the neighbors realizing he was there, so he groped his way around in utter darkness and a state of panic, trying to find a window, colliding with chairs, a sofa. Something fell onto the floor and broke, making a sharp, shattering sound that caused him to whip around in the dark, terrified. He felt as if a shadow had just passed, brushing against him. He was exhausted from the trip and had a chill; he hadn't had dinner. He thought his parents were probably hysterical, might have called the police, thought Anita wouldn't be able to sleep that night. The house was damp, and when he got into bed, the sheets and blankets felt almost wet. Aunt Eli's smell was still strong, a stale, sweet smell, like cinnamon or an alcoholic's sweat. He piled on several blankets, still fully clothed, and curled into a ball, trying to get warm. He'd never felt so miserable in all his life, or so fragile, or so guilt-ridden, but something inside him remained steadfast, as though each movement he made were a quiet rejoinder—*I want this, I choose to be here.* He fell asleep. A blank, terrifying sleep, extremely deep, imageless. In the darkness, the yellowy light of a streetlamp filtered through a hole in the broken blinds like a needle, glimmering.

He rose at dawn, starving, and inspected the house. Opening the blinds just the tiniest bit, he recalled the summer day he'd been there with Anita. It seemed almost comical that he'd been so scared the night before; it was just the same old house he remembered from that summer, with a huge, kitsch painting of the aqueduct in Segovia, little porcelain souvenirs, photos of his uncle, his parents, even one of him and Anita. It moved him now in a way it never had before, as if Aunt Eli's life were still there, resting, infused in each of the things that had once been hers, and he got the feeling, for the first time, that he was experiencing an exclusively female world. He felt like he could see thousands of tiny emotional threads connecting all of those things, attached to the *Great Women of History* collection on the bookshelf, contained within the immaculate kitchen, tucked into the slightly sunken, green sofa on which she'd arranged a crocheted doily in the guise of an armrest, to hide a wine stain. Aunt Eli's life, in that house, was a mental state, a whirlwind of supremely concentrated details. It made him feel sorry not to have loved her more.

Walking through town, he got the same feeling he'd had at Aunt Eli's. The morning was sunny but still cold, a damp cold that seemed to radiate upward from the ground. Almost all of the shops were closed, and the estuary looked kind of dirty—full of algae, sticks, a few plastic bottles that the tide had dragged in. It was as though some great misfortune had befallen the town, a plague or a siege, as though the people who'd lived there had fought viciously and then given up, the way primitive peoples gave up when their fields were burned down or an invading army took over and forced their citizens into slavery. Those remaining had a slightly pensive, defeated air—survivors of the shipwreck—but the same lassitude as in summer, a lassitude that now seemed not festive but indolent.

It took him several hours to ascertain, after having asked half a dozen people, where he might find a school for developmentally disabled kids. He was sent to the regular high school, in the end, and there he discovered, thanks to the secretary, that the classes for those kids were held at another location, in rooms the local council had provided clear on the other side of town. Day had broken fully, and in the sun, at least, it was actually a little warm. He felt a moment of something akin to nervous glee on his way there. It was time for the students to start school. He watched them in the distance, a colorful silhouette, about twenty people in all. What he saw was so different from what he'd imagined that he hesitated a bit as he approached. All of the students were about his age, though some were younger, but they seemed to have vastly different disabilities. Some were clearly withdrawn and silent, others shrieking; it seemed kids with Down's syndrome were mixed in with others who were mildly autistic. He'd never seen so many mentally disabled kids in the same place before and wasn't prepared for the speed and noise and fury with which they seemed to live. The false joy he'd felt as he got closer vanished immediately, replaced by a sense of horror and insecurity, a feeling of intense ridiculousness. He stepped into the warm, compact group swirling around the entrance, feeling the contact of mothers on either side of him, of adolescents running beside him. Suddenly he became self-absorbed. Not a daydream but a sort of vague, confused, fluctuating evocation. It was as if all of those women and all of those teenagers had lost their individual characteristics, the things that made them concrete and definable, and for a moment all gave off one common scent. Finally he asked one of the teachers about Marita.

"You're her brother, right?"

And without knowing why, he replied, "Yes."

"It's a disgrace," she said. "That girl only shows up when she feels like it. And it's your fault—yours and your parents'."

He didn't see her once, despite the fact that he spent the entire day walking all over town in the hopes of happening upon her at any moment. He knew he'd stand a better chance of finding her if he went over toward the boxy houses by the estuary, but he was afraid of running into Pablo, Marcos, Tejas, or Rivero. He felt ridiculous, and nervous. His states of mind jostled, overlapping one another like absolute states with no shading or gradations—anxiety, tedium, embarrassment, concern for his parents. Sometimes they formed a sort of parenthesis around his mind, which would go blank, and he'd feel something like a caving-in, and sorrow; that was the one harsh, constant sensation of the day. The only thing that slightly consoled him was knowing that those were the same streets Marita walked, the same people she would pass if she went out, the same trees, the same estuary, the same ground she walked on.

He ate lunch by himself and then went out to the dunes. He wanted to go back, to see—even if it was just one last time—the place where it had all taken place, but finding it was less straightforward than he'd imagined. He remembered where they'd first seen her, so he went there and then tried to reconstruct the route they'd taken. The estuary smelled bad that afternoon and the tide was high, the sky had clouded over again. After two hours the whole town was deprived of light and had become a mildly spiritless, hostile place, less real than when it was sunny. It disconcerted him not to be able to find the spot, but all he could remember clearly was a slightly bowed pine tree and a clearing in the sand with some low brush. The dunes were full of places that could have been that place, but each one had some detail that left him unsure. He did, however, find the place he'd been with Frani that first night; he saw the stump she had sat on, and he stayed there for a few minutes. At times it seemed as though all of the dunes, as one, were furling and unfurling around him, like some dreamlike sequence in a children's story.

He walked back to town feeling a keen wistfulness for his house, his parents, Anita. He supposed that at that time of day, the three of them would be home, waiting for him to turn up, calling his friends, and that they wouldn't sleep that night and wouldn't have slept the night before. How many times would they have read his note by that point? Ten times? A hundred? Searching continuously for some sign, interpreting and reinterpreting as if each sentence were pregnant with meaning, with valuable information. He regretted not having written it in a more soothing tone. It started to drizzle. He went back to Aunt Eli's.

It was an endless evening, an endless night, and when the light was finally all the way gone, the house scared him once more. He heard sounds he didn't recognize, sounds coming from the kitchen. He actually said aloud, "There's someone in the house."

He didn't know if he said it in an attempt to keep it from being true or to make it true. In the darkness, he tried to think of Marita. Even that suddenly seemed strange—the idea of Marita. He'd constructed for himself, over the course of those two months, an idea of Marita that might have nothing to do with the real Marita; he'd invented her in a haphazard fashion, through trial and error, and made of her a mold. And the mere fact of having spent one day in that town in autumn had eroded a bit of his constructed truth, and what's more, seen now in its *true* light, he wasn't even sure his trip actually made any sense. He saw himself as if he were standing in an imaginary doorway, his hair ridiculously combed, smiling, holding out a bouquet of flowers nobody asked for, offering them to a girl who, in all likelihood, would run away if she saw him. Having the actual town as a backdrop nullified his fantasy, immediately coarsened it, subjected it to rules unknown to him. What exactly was he planning to do when he saw her? When he asked himself that, not in his imagination but actually asked aloud, trying to make the image as true as possible, he heard a sort of old-timey pantomime music, and felt an almost childish fear that would not be able to offset her real face, her real breasts, her lips—a fear that everything that was the *true* Marita would stifle the impulse that had made him come down from Madrid to begin with, the urge that, from a distance, had seemed so pressing. The whole night was charged with the senseless sensation that something that had never before taken place was going to occur, something his imagination could never even have begun to imagine during the daytime.

"There she is," he said to himself, his heart in his throat, "*right there.*"

It was nearly dark, and he'd spent that whole second day wandering around town searching for her, first diligently, then dejectedly. He'd been on the verge of going to a call shop to phone home but then promptly realized they'd be able to figure out where he was from the phone number. It was almost nighttime again, and a little cold. The damp had given him a chill, and he thought that if he didn't get back to Aunt Eli's, he'd end up getting sick.

She was sitting on a little bench in front of the supermarket, two or three plastic bags at her feet, staring at the automatic door as it opened and closed, as though she were waiting for someone. He wasn't even sure it was her until he got a few feet closer. She was wearing a brown, corduroy skirt and a blue sweater with a huge cat face embroidered on the front, her hair was longer and pulled back in a ponytail that was too high, almost on the very top of her head. She was so ugly it embarrassed him, embarrassed him in a compassionate and almost painful way—the same way he'd occasionally felt when someone he cared about made a fool of themselves in front of people who'd be harsh and judgmental about it. Autumn had passed over her, as it had everyone, and yet rather than being affected the way others were, she seemed bizarrely removed, exhibiting the simpleminded rusticity of a country girl. Her eyes were much smaller than he remembered; they were different eyes, diminutive, like thin, horizontal lines, two notches cut into the rough skin of her face. His heart began to pound furiously, and he thought his voice was going to tremble the second he opened his mouth. He was absolutely certain it was all going to be a complete failure. He took several steps toward her and then stopped, daunted. He didn't know where to start. She turned to him.

"Hello."

"Hello."

But nothing on her face altered.

"Do you remember me?"

And then he got the feeling that something was spilling over her expression, spreading through and filling it, like a cloud of milk in a cup of tea. Seriousness settled onto her face and then turned inward, something within her was collapsing noisily, but her insides continued silent and static.

"Yes," she replied gravely, "you're the boy from summer."

"I came down from Madrid."

His legs began to tremble. The two of them were in a slightly awkward position—she was still sitting, he was standing beside her. In a way his nervousness felt akin to falling asleep; suddenly he saw a different landscape, a different planet, one on which everything was unreal, with the exception of Marita.

"Why?"

"Because I wanted to see you."

He bore the weight of that silence for a second, gathering his strength, and thought, *Now I'll tell her everything.* And then, immediately afterward, *Tell her . . . what?* Marita didn't seem surprised by the news, but nor did she seem indifferent. It was impossible to know what was going on inside her head.

"Did your aunt die?"

"Yeah, she died in the end."

"Poor thing."

And then more silence, which Marita broke.

"Frani's not here. She left town."

"I didn't come for Frani, I came to see you."

"Me?"

"Yeah, about what happened this summer."

"Oh, that."

And the oddest thing—it was as though she were suddenly disappointed, or ashamed, about something. Not something to do with him, but herself. He got the sense that she had resigned herself, and that that was normal behavior for her, part of her character, as if she simply took certain events and meticulously wrapped them in brown paper and then deposited them on shelves in something like a basement.

"But you didn't do anything."

He thought he was going to cry. He clenched his jaw as hard as he could; he'd have liked to break his teeth. And after a silence, Marita insisted.

"You didn't hurt me."

Her intellect seemed to be racing through an enormous space at dizzying speed, and he thought that adapting to her, to Marita, must be like adapting to that motionless speed, like a gyroscope's. She began twisting the handles on the plastic bags, glancing at the supermarket entrance. She'd hung her head, and since he was still standing, he couldn't see her face. Marita's shoulders were tense and burly, her spine slightly curved. He placed a hand on her shoulder, and she leaned forward. To him it was like a punishment for her to do that. But then she immediately stood, leaping up all at once, and made for a woman just emerging from the supermarket with several shopping bags, a woman who looked to be about forty.

"Help me, don't just stand there like an imbecile."

Marita took the bags.

She was a graceless woman, lusterless, and ugly in a way that was foreign to him and would probably remain foreign to him for the rest of his life, as though it had taken three generations to reach such extremes of ugliness. She looked very much like a man, her body overly stocky, but she had two spindly little legs that splayed as she walked, the tips of her toes pointing slightly outward.

"Who's this?" she asked Marita directly, not even glancing at him. "A friend of yours?"

"No, a boy from summer."

"My name is Tomás," he said without anyone having asked, finding his voice.

"Yes, Tomás."

"Come on, get a move on."

"I'm leaving for Madrid tomorrow."

The woman had already begun walking.

"OK," Marita replied, taking the bags and trailing after her without looking back.

The memory begins there, when he wakes, when he looks into the mirror in the bathroom with no running water at Aunt Eli's. He's gone three days without showering and smells bad. Never in all his life has he smelled that bad, because never in all his life has he gone three days without showering; it's an acrid smell, thick, one that he almost doesn't recognize as coming from his own body, and it makes him feel a little bit ashamed. He tries to be reasonable, standing before that image, but when he moves he gets the sense that he should have done something else, without being exactly sure what. His chest moves out of sync with his breathing; like a tree trunk driven vertically into the mud, his balance is precarious. And he puts on his shirt and pants and packs everything he brought into his backpack to return to Madrid. Suddenly he's relieved at the thought of going back to Madrid, he feels an expansive giddiness, nudging him back toward the side of life where he belongs, a whirlwind of jitters. He thinks about Anita and how he doesn't know what his parents' reactions are going to be. They'll most likely punish him, but he can handle the punishment. Grounded for four months, six months, a year, he doesn't really care. That kind of punishment befits his world, has been made for him, it can't hurt him, he thinks in a kind of sad way.

The memory picks back up at the station, where he learns that the afternoon bus doesn't leave for five hours (he missed the morning one by just five minutes), and then on the streets again, where he walks around. Is that when it occurs to him that he could, maybe, go to the entrance of Marita's school? He's not sure. There's a gap in his memory, a billowy lacuna, like a bank of pillows.

The walk to Marita's school seems shorter than the first time, and when he spots the same doorway as the day before, there's something different about it—a sort of fluttery, festive jubilation. The girls and boys look like they're wearing costumes, and they're all accompanied by parents and siblings. It's a costume party. Once he's standing before them, he's sure. There are four different princesses—two in pale pink, one in sky blue, and the other in some questionable shade of white—all so overexcited at their princessdom that they seem to find no end to their glee, ever delighted and delightful; a pirate with an open vest and a skull tattoo on his chest, scratching at his eye patch; a cardboard robot; and even a bag of candy in a see-through suit filled with colored balloons. But the most elaborate and original costume is one worn by a girl with a vacant air, about fifteen years old, standing beside her mother amid that whirlwind of costumes, dressed as a tube of toothpaste. She's even wearing a round, red hat, as the cap. She's been told to say, "Brush your teeth three times a day, once after every meal."

And she repeats it each time someone comes up and says *what a nice costume,* more an alarming, apocalyptic proclamation than a personal hygiene recommendation.

It's strange—in the memory, at first, he has no sense that he's searching for Marita. He's simply there, sort of mawkishly moved. It's as if all those boys and girls, so ecstatic to be in costume that they're out of control, were imbued with the unusual, silvery hues of a life unknown; their breathing sounds a bit like grunting at times, as if he were weaving through a swing set, and their faces are complex and beautiful. Contemplating the joy and excitement of others has always intrigued him, it's like something private being put on display. And then suddenly, in the memory, Marita is back. The fantastical thing about the memory is its far-fetched sense of suspense. He becomes anxious, this time as if breathing noxious air, as if life were bent on placing him over and over again before something he was required to work his way through, a swamp, a murky and definitely unsolvable place—Marita. And behind that swamp lay the world—true stories, real days. She, too, stands a few feet apart, watching all the children. She's not in costume, and is alone. She walks up to one of the princesses and grabs the train of her dress. He approaches her. There is a fleeting conversation that may in actual fact have been longer and more involved but in the memory was quite schematic.

"You didn't go to Madrid?"

"Not yet, this afternoon."

"Oh."

And suddenly an urge to be with her makes him ask, almost excitedly, "Do you like costumes?"

"Yes. Well, not all of them. *That* one, for example, I can't *stand*," she almost yells, pointing at the toothpaste.

"But you didn't bring a costume."

"I didn't know there was a party."

He has an idea.

"How about if we ask your teacher? We might be able to borrow one."

And Marita says, "If you'll stay here with me."

He's not sure why, but he feels an odd sort of heartache. Something physical has happened beneath his flesh, his skin, his eyelids, an imperceptible twitch in the corner of Marita's mouth, and his, too, as if the two of them shared a reason to live. He's shocked to discover this small facet of Marita's—she doesn't want anyone to know she came alone. A diminutive shame, folded up into a crease of flesh, intimate and human and not malicious in the slightest. He gives her a clammy hand. He thinks, *This is what I was supposed to do.*

"There's a trunk full of clothes somewhere, things from the Christmas pageant," the teacher says when they go ask her.

And there they are, in the memory—Marita and him, standing before a tangled wad of costumes in a trunk.

"What do you want to dress up as?"

"A ninja."

"There is no ninja."

"What is there?"

This is the first time he gazes at Marita's face without looking away, as she contemplates the trunk they've been rummaging through. It is, perhaps, the clearest image in the entire memory—Marita's face bent over a trunk full of costumes. It's a hard image, full of skin and fear and eyelashes, as though someone had struck her in the face and then slipped away into a crowd unpunished, as if that had always been predestined—it would be thus, and no one could do anything to stop it. Marita's face, full of sounds. It is there that he discovers her *hardness*, just as he one day discovered the hardness in Pablo, Marcos, Tejas, and Rivero—an odd, clever sort of torpor inuring them to life. "There's a shepherd," he finally says.

"Is there a devil?"

"No, there's no devil, either. There's a Roman soldier."

And Marita says then, gravely, "A Roman soldier."

Is that really the memory? Is Marita-the-Roman-soldier the memory, or is the memory actually more like sorrow, something that subsides and then is roused once more, like an appeased mob? Is there really a porch where they all play drop the hanky, or is the real memory the shock, the excitement behind the handkerchief and behind himself, even, when the bag of candy trips and falls on her face to great collective concern? The memory both is and is not a lie; he sees that, he will see it.

Dressed as a Roman soldier, Marita takes on new grace, and he has an absurd thought: *All I have to do is find out who she is.* A Roman soldier with a plastic breastplate and a bent sword leading a battalion of grown-up shadows. A Roman soldier whose panties show when she bends over.

"Do you want to meet my boyfriend?" she asks.

"Of course."

The pirate-boyfriend. And then she confides to him in an aside, "I don't like him."

"Why not?"

"I like normal boys."

And just in case he didn't get it, she adds, "Normal boys like you."

They make their way through that game, in the memory, the Roman soldier and him. Is that the game? Pretending not to pick up on Marita-the-Roman-soldier's flirting, or is it turning his gaze upward and suddenly seeing the day shining down vertically beneath a wide-open sky? Underneath the memory, from that second on, is a magenta-colored flame, like a subterranean river, something darkened.

"I've always liked normal boys, but they don't like me."

It's not a heavy-hearted profession but a sweet, oafish statement of fact, like saying *It's daytime out.* He gives her his hand once more. Five fingers, thick and strong, like those of a grown man.

Various scenes from the memory collide in a granular light, overlapping, piling on top of one another until an almost animal sort of presence emerges. Not seeing Marita's face as clearly as before helps him understand it better. It's become a state, an actual presence. He sees that in her own way, she's proud, because when a game is being played, she uses her physical strength (she's stronger than the others) to assert herself. He sees that she lives entirely unprotected, and that inside her brain there are dead-end labyrinths where she sometimes gets lost, like a girl collapsing in a sudden fit of desperation, as if telling herself, out of fear, that *there's nothing there*. And there is no hope, but nor is there sorrow, just a teenager concentrating very hard on being nothing. A small, round nothing. He understands, too, that each part of Marita's personality reveals a great capacity for attention, that she observes everything with care, and that he himself has become, for Marita, an object of wonder, because when his shoelace comes undone and he bends down to tie it, she says, "Let me do it, I tie laces very well."

And she makes a double knot, too tight, lingering over it, as though wanting to savor the scene and keep it for herself.

The morning is long, with time enough for many games. In some, the families participate, partnering up with the kids; in others the children play alone and the families look on. Marita is different from the others in a peculiar way—for her, the fun of the game resides solely in being observed, so if he stops watching, she stops playing. And as he's watching her play a game in which they have to run to carry balls from one basket to another on the opposite side of the schoolyard, it occurs to him that he knows her, pure and simple, he knows her as well as if he'd spent many afternoons like this by her side. She comes running back to him and hugs him. Her Roman-soldier body transmits its heat, its heartbeat, its physical strength. He doesn't have to say anything to her in order to save her, all he has to do is believe in her, in the change in the air, in her gruff hand that yanks his up obstinately to make the sign of champions. He laughs. Later he'll wonder if all solace is like that, but in the memory the thing that stands out is simply the end of sorrow.

And sometimes in the memory, he also senses that *her* memory of the horror is far more certain and fixed than his, and that despite it all, she's able to carry on, as though floating in silence. When the students are made to draw pictures, he sits beside her, and she rests her head on his shoulder, a heavy head, which she lays down and then lifts up, as though it were rebounding off something soft, and then rests back down once more.

"It's for you, the drawing."

A woman and a dog, simple and violent, done in green, like a stain on the paper. And that's when it occurs to him that he loves her.

Or it's later, perhaps, when he looks at the clock and thinks he's going to miss the bus and says, "I have to go, Marita."
And she replies, "No."

Or in the last half hour, when Marita accompanies him to the bus station, still dressed as a Roman soldier because she refused to take off her costume.
"I'll go back for my clothes tomorrow; I want them to see me dressed like this at home."
And they walk through the pine grove between the town hall and the bus station, her leaning into him, in silence.

Or at the last second, when he doesn't know what to do with her face, so huge, so full of life, round as a pie, so close to his as they stand there by the bus, which is already full of people staring at them through the glass, and Marita says, "I'd be so happy if you were my boyfriend."

That and the terrible urge, each time the memory surfaces, to turn back time, to become two, three, fifteen years younger, to go back to that bus station where a naïve teenage boy is hugging a girl dressed up as a Roman soldier. He waves a hand and it's as if the physical sensation itself dissolves, as if it were made of multiple tiny particles, some more alive than others, a rain both driving and still, a cascade of unconnected sensations in which one desire burns like a red-hot ember, reaching out to him, shaking him, shouting in his ear—*Kiss her, you idiot, kiss her.*

ABOUT THE AUTHOR

ANDRÉS BARBA MUÑIZ (Madrid, 1975) is a Spanish novelist, essayist, translator, scriptwriter and photographer. He is the author of a total of twelve books of literary fiction, non-fiction, photography, arts and children's literature. Among other prizes he has been awarded the Premio Torrente Ballester de Narrativa (for *Versiones de Teresa*), the Premio Anagrama de Ensayo (for *La ceremonia del porno*) and the Premio Juan March de Narrativa (for *Muerte de un caballo*). He was also shortlisted in the XIX Premio Herralde de Novela (for *La hermana de Katia*, made into a film a few years after by Mijke de Jong). In 2010 he was featured in Granta's magazine as one of the twenty-two best young Spanish-language writers. His works have been translated into ten languages.

ABOUT THE TRANSLATOR

LISA DILLMAN translates from the Spanish and Catalan and teaches at Emory University in Atlanta. In addition to *Rain Over Madrid*, by Andrés Barba, some of her recent translations include *The Mule*, by Juan Eslava Galán, *Me, Who Dove Into the Heart of the World*, by Sabina Berman, Christopher Domínguez *Michael's Critical Dictionary of Mexican Literature* and Yuri Herrera's *Signs Preceding the End of the World*.

DISCARD

CPSIA information can be obtained at www.ICGtesting.com
Printed in the USA
LVOW06s2237180915

454793LV00001B/1/P